DAMAGE CONTROL

A BUCKNER THRILLER SUSPENSE

KATHY BENNETT

To those who bear the scars of sexual abuse and rise above the trauma to carry on another day.

Know that others respect you and are moved by your strength.

<u>*A Deadly Beauty*</u> – *(Book 5)*

A beauty pageant is terrorized when a contestant is killed, and another woman goes missing. Maddie Divine investigates, while two more girls disappear.

<u>*A Deadly Prayer*</u> – *A Novella (Book 6)*

Maddie Divine teams up with fellow Detective Gunner Ferrari to elicit facts amid secrets, deceit, and greed—all revolving around a charismatic preacher and his celebrated church.

<u>*A Deadly Blood Moon*</u> – *(Book 7)*

Maddie Divine receives an urgent call from her father-in-law's senior facility—he's vanished. Can Maddie unmask a deadly conspiracy before the wicked claim her badge and her loved one's life?

<u>*The Deadly Boxed Set*</u> – *(Books 1-3)*

Get a deal on *A Dozen Deadly Roses, A Deadly Blessing, and A Deadly Justice.*

THE BUCKNER THRILLER SUSPENSE SERIES

(A Trilogy)

<u>*Collateral Damage*</u> – *(Book 1)*

When Amber Buckner gets kidnapped, she tries to stay one step ahead of her captor until her cop husband can find her. What she doesn't know is her husband isn't looking for her—no one is—the psycho has seen to that.

<u>*Damaged Goods*</u> *– (Book 2)*

Roy Buckner and his female partner investigate a cold-case cop killing. They trigger and uncover a trail of secrets that may end everyone's career—if not their lives.

<u>*Damage Control*</u> *- (Book 3)*

A depraved pimp lures two young girls to Los Angeles, while divorcing cops call a truce while hunting a serial kidnapper. Can good conquer evil before the innocents are sold to the highest bidder?

DAMAGE CONTROL

PROLOGUE

ROY

"Are you sure this is what you want?"

Roy Buckner gave a reluctant shrug with one shoulder. "I don't have much say in the matter. Amber decided she wants a divorce. I can't *make* her stay married to me."

The lawyer glanced at the papers before him, then glared at Roy. "Yeah, but you don't need to bend over for her either." He shook his head. "You're being extremely generous."

Roy sighed. "It's my fault—"

The litigator held up his hand. "I know, I know. You screwed another woman, your wife found out, left you, and so it's all your fault." He crossed his arms on the desk, leaning closer. "I've been handling cop divorces for well over a decade. In my experience, it takes two people to break a marriage." He grimaced and sat back. "Heap on what the two of you went through the last couple of years…" he shrugged. "Why give her the house, child support, plus pay for her car?" The counselor leveled his gaze on Roy. "You'll be living in a cardboard box on Skid Row trying to pay for all of that—or kill yourself working overtime and off-duty jobs. She's got a good job with good pay and benefits." The attorney shook his head again. "If you ask me, you're making a foolish decision."

Roy flashed a wry smile. "Foolish decisions seem to be my forte. No sense in changing things now."

PART I

1

AMBER

Tick. Tick. Tick.

As the early morning sun came through the window, Amber Buckner listened to the metronome-like beats from the clock on her shrink's desk. They mirrored the beat of her heart.

"I think I made a mistake leaving Roy."

Doctor Angela Stevens glanced at the yellow legal pad on her lap. "You've been separated for what…eighteen months?"

"Yes," Amber said, nodding.

The psychologist crossed her legs. "So why, after a year and a half, are you reconsidering your decision?"

"I've had time to reassess everything—the Seth Farley situation, me becoming a cop, and Roy's affair."

"Okay, and how has that reevaluation changed your view?"

"I realized I was doing what was best for me, but what about Gage? He's only three. He needs his daddy."

"There are plenty of children growing up in single-parent homes, and they turn out just fine."

"Many don't!" She clenched her teeth and shook her head. "Maybe I acted too fast." She sighed and cast her gaze around the room, as if the answer was in a corner somewhere, then returned her focus to her shrink. "Being a cop changes your perspective…of everything. Before my kidnapping, I faced plenty of pressure. As a Neo-natal ICU nurse, I had physicians yelling, mother's panicking, babies stopped breathing…I often made life and death decisions. And that stress was real and critical."

She readjusted the pillow under her left arm. "When I graduated from the police academy, I knew interacting with the public would be stressful, frustrating, and dangerous, but I didn't realize how much of the frustration, mental strain, and anxiety would come from inside the department. A cop in today's world is in a no-win situation."

She looked into the other woman's eyes. "I feel some compassion for Seth Farley. He thought the LAPD had wronged him. It wasn't true, but now, with my experience as an officer, I can see how he might have perceived he was a target." She rubbed her hands together. "My whole family still suffers from the ordeal." She blew out a breath, relieved she'd been able to articulate her thoughts.

The doctor nodded. "Okay. How does all of that relate to any uncertainty about leaving your husband?"

"Because, now that I wear a badge, I understand he needed…relief."

The other woman smiled. "Do you think all police officers who face extreme stress, or hardships on the job and in their personal life, need relationships outside of their marriage to cope?"

"I can't speak for them. I only know Roy is a decent man. Yes, he cheated on me. He said it was only twice, and I think he's being truthful. I wasn't available to him sexually, and he found someone who was. His partner was hurting as much as he was—for different reasons, but Katie was just as damaged. She was willing to be intimate, while I rejected him. I don't like it, but I understand why it happened. I've forgiven him, and I want him back."

"Will you have an issue trusting him?"

"Absolutely. I'll need your help." Amber gave the doctor a crooked smile. "And…that's why you make the big bucks."

2

———

ROY

On Thursday morning, Roy Buckner moved with purpose. He wasn't used to having his three-year-old son on a workday. "Okay, buddy, finish your cereal and apple slices. We've got to get going. Daddy will be late for work.

The little boy clutched a handful of oat circles and jammed the contents of his hand against his open lips. Most of the pieces fell onto the table.

"Good job, son." He smiled. "Don't be afraid to use your fingers to put the cereal into your mouth."

Gage reached for his sippy cup and swallowed several gulps of milk. He grinned, then grabbed a fruit slice and bit off a piece.

"You keep eating. Daddy has to brush his teeth and grab a tie."

Half an hour later, they were on their way to the three-year-old's preschool. As they slogged through morning traffic, he pointed out yellow buses packed with children, sleek sports cars, and crossing guards shepherding youngsters through the vehicles.

"Poweece," Gage said, pointing at a black-and-white ahead in the lane next to them.

"That's right, son. Those officers probably just came on duty, and they'll be working the whole day—even past the time Mommy comes and gets you."

From his safety of his car seat, the toddler clapped his hands.

"Mommy will pick you up this afternoon. You'll spend the night with her, and then Daddy will come for you tomorrow morning. How does that sound?" Roy glanced at his youngster in the rearview mirror.

The little boy nodded.

As he pulled into the parking lot of the school, he wondered how the screwy schedule he and his estranged wife maintained affected their son.

Roy felt better after walking his son to class, when Gage threw his arms around his father's legs, tilted his head up for a kiss, and as soon as he finished, ran to join a group of kids building a tower of wooden blocks.

Back in his pickup truck, knowing his son was safe and happy, Roy shifted his thoughts to his caseload of sex offender registrants.

Over the past four months, three young boys had disappeared from the San Fernando Valley. His position as the coordinator over the department's Sexual Assault Units, had made him the logical first stop, and he'd asked the detectives working Missing Persons to meet with him.

Hopefully, between them, they would have some good ideas for finding the boys.

3

———

DAZZLE

Monroe Peck, AKA Dazzle McDaddy, rubbed his hand over his face trying to energize his brain for the long drive back to Los Angeles.

Looking in the rearview mirror, he watched eleven-year-old Brooke Desmond take a bite of the In-N-Out burger he'd bought her just north of Salt Lake City.

The girl sat in the backseat of his black Escalade, while Payton, her fourteen-year-old sister, sat up front next to him shoving french fries into her mouth.

He gave the older girl a sidelong glance. "You might want to go a little easier on those fries. They pack on the pounds."

She dropped the crispy strips into the cardboard box holding her hamburger and the remaining greasy potatoes.

"Yes. You're right. I've just never had a hamburger or fries that tasted so good."

Dazzle looked into his rearview mirror again. "What about you, little one? Do you like your burger?"

The little girl nodded and took a sip of soda.

Neither girl said much, and after the carb overload wore off, they were fast asleep.

Traveling south on I-15 through Utah, the least-populated portion of the trip, Dazzle struggled to keep his eyes open. As tired as he was, he knew he couldn't stop. He had to get to Vegas, and then LA.

He'd left the rest of his girls in a motel on Flamingo Road on the east side of Vegas. He'd been gone too long.

Who knew what kind of trouble a bunch of unsupervised whores could create?

They were about a half hour outside of Cedar City when Payton woke up. A huge yawn contorted her face.

He frowned.

Brooke's eyes fluttered open as well.

That one is the moneymaker. He used the rearview mirror to smile at the younger girl. "It won't be long, and we'll be out of Utah and into Nevada. I told you girls I'd show you a good time, and there isn't a better place to have fun than in Las Vegas."

Brooke rubbed the sleep from her eyes. "When do we get to go home?"

"Home? Why would you want to go home? I'm taking you to one of the most exciting places on Earth. I'm taking you to Las Vegas." He grinned. "I'll take you to Circus Circus, and at New York-New York they have a cool roller coaster to ride. It'll be a ton of fun. You'll see."

In the passenger seat, Payton turned toward him. "Do you think we can play some slot machines? One time, a girl from school got all dressed up like a grownup, and she got to play some slots before the security guards made her leave."

"No. Not this trip. Sometimes my business takes me to Vegas," he said, glancing at Payton. "Of course, I'd want you to come with me."

As he knew she would, the girl beamed.

He looked over his shoulder at the young one. "I'd want you to come, too."

Unlike her sister, Brooke didn't look thrilled.

That's okay, little one. He wasn't worried. He'd bring her along slow. Eventually, they all came around…one way or the other.

4

———

ROBYN

Robyn McGee bustled down the long hallway of her white French chateau in lower Bel Air Estates —a gated enclave of the rich and famous in Los Angeles. She carried several bags of boys' clothing and toys.

Behind her, the weekly housekeeper, laden with two large bundles of bedding, struggled to keep up.

"Rosa, I can't wait for you to see the room the props department built for the little boy I've adopted. Logan will arrive in the next few days, and there's so much to do!"

"I'm so…happy…for you…Miss Robyn," the housekeeper said, while trying to catch her breath.

They entered the guest bedroom that had been transformed into a train enthusiast's wonderland. Rosa set her burdens down. "Oh, this is *magnifico*. What a treat for a young boy." She moved toward the bed, shaped and crafted like a train locomotive and rubbed her hand on the bright blue wood. Beneath the bunk were two drawers on each side, with rounded facings painted to resemble locomotive wheels.

"Did you notice how they designed a mural on the wall to appear like the train is coming out of a tunnel?" Robyn asked.

"The room is magical. I'm sure your new son will be very happy." The maid pulled the bedding from the bags. "I'll get these sheets and bedspread in the washer and have the room ready before leaving today."

Robyn dumped jeans and shirts adorned with dinosaurs onto the mattress and began pulling off tags. "Do you have time to wash his news clothes, too? I don't know how much he's bringing from the foster home."

"Of course, miss. We'll have everything ready for Logan."

"Excellent." She glanced at her watch. "I've got to go to my office. I have a conference call with a couple of actors."

"I can finish this. You go on ahead."

With a curt nod, Robyn strode down the hallway to the other side of the residence.

After winning back-to-back Oscars for casting two Best Picture films, she'd allowed herself to splurge, and bought the chateau. The home was gigantic for a woman alone, but if you wanted to stay on the Hollywood A-list, you had to live like a star.

She entered her office through the door attached to the butler's pantry. She worked from home, which was just as well. Traffic was horrendous, and the streets were filled with the homeless and criminals. Today, her business would be conducted by phone.

She'd had the office built out of two bedrooms at the far end of the house. At her request, the architect had designed a separate entrance, so thespian hopefuls weren't traipsing through her home.

A-listers were always welcomed into her private quarters. Dime-a-dozen hack actors were not.

Robyn flipped on lights, and opened the blinds, then poked her head outside, and waved at the gardener who wore hearing protection against the whine of his leaf blower.

He powered the machine to a low idle and dislodged his earmuffs to hear her.

"Apague su máquina. Es muy ruidoso." Her knowledge of basic Spanish allowed her to communicate with the help and let him know to turn off his noisy equipment.

"Lo siento mucho, señorita."

Good. He'd turn it off. She wanted to be sure she could hear her caller. She smiled and nodded at the groundsman and shut the door.

5

ROY

Roy pulled his truck into a parking space several blocks away from the LAPD's headquarters, known as PAB—or the Police Administration Building. When he was first assigned to Robbery Homicide Division, he welcomed the walk from his vehicle to his desk as easy exercise. But that was almost two years ago.

Today, the sidewalks were overtaken by tents, cardboard boxes, and sleeping bags. Los Angeles was the homeless capital of the country—those who were destitute flocked to the moderate weather of the southland.

Homeless transients he'd interviewed over the years had admitted that their local police departments in the Midwest and northeast had bought them bus tickets to the land of perennial sunshine and free handouts—namely Los Angeles.

Once inside, Roy swiped his ID card to gain access to

the upper floors and into the section of the fifth-floor housing RHD. He walked the length of the room to his small office. The glorified walk-in closet held a desk and little else—as long as you didn't count the piles of paper and stacked files.

The LAPD firmly believed in the saying, *do more with less.*

As the city's Sexual Assault Crime Coordinator, he worked closely with the twenty-one sex crime detectives at the outlying police stations. He received all crime and arrest reports regarding sex crimes and coordinated with those detectives on their investigations watching for similar crimes in different communities throughout city.

Roy was also in charge of the REACT team, which monitored and enforced compliance of sex offenders who'd been ordered by the court to register. Those tasks were also handled by the sex crime detectives, and that was on top of their sexual assault crime cases.

With human sexual trafficking spiking, the thin blue line of sex crimes investigators and the tracking of sexual offenders was stretched as tight as a freshly donned condom.

But it had been the missing young boys that had Roy calling the sex crimes detectives from Valley Bureau and reserving a conference room, because there was no way he and the sex detectives would fit into his shoebox office.

He grabbed his coffee mug and went to the cubicle used as a coffee klatch.

Roy stuffed a dollar into the piggybank prominently displayed beside the creamer, then poured his brew and left it black.

When he returned to his office, his phone was ringing. "Detective Buckner, how may I help you?"

"By gettin' your ass out to the lobby and letting us in," responded a gruff voice.

Roy recognized the tone of the Valley Bureau Sexual Assault Crimes and REACT coordinator. "I'll be right there. We're using one of the conference rooms in the main corridor."

"Well, hurry up. There's about ten of us standing around with our thumbs up our ass."

Before he could respond, the line disconnected. Roy was sure the detective's condescending demands were for the benefit and enjoyment of the other detectives in the RHD lobby. They were no doubt pissed they had to carpool and convoy all the way to PAB.

He took a sip from his mug and strolled toward the lobby.

6

———

AMBER

In the late afternoon, Amber stepped into the playroom of Gage's nursery school. Her gaze scanned the children playing with stacking toys and magnetized tiles. Finally, she spied her son. He was pushing a firetruck on the floor while making siren sounds.

As if sensing her arrival, he stopped playing and looked toward the door.

"Mama!" He pushed himself up and ran toward her.

She went to her knees and held out her arms.

He threw himself at her, almost knocking her over.

"I guess you missed me, huh?"

He gazed into her eyes and nodded.

She grinned. "I miss you every time I'm not with you."

She rose, signed out, and told him to say goodbye to his

teacher. Afterward, she took his hand and they walked to the car together where she got him situated in his car seat.

Driving home, she asked him about his day at school and if he'd had a good time with his father the previous night. As she did, a pang of guilt washed over her. It was her fault that her son was juggled between households on various nights of the week.

"We play. He reads me book."

She smiled. "He loves you, Gage. Just as much as I do." She glanced into the rearview mirror, then swallowed hard before asking, "Uh, does Daddy ever have any friends over?" She checked the mirror again as Gage shook his head. *You're horrible. Do not use your son to spy on Roy.* "Do you remember why Daddy picked you up and took you to school this morning?"

Another shake of his head.

"Mommy had to go to court. She had to testify that a bad man had stolen a car."

"Why?"

"The bad man said he needed a ride and his friend had let him use the car. That was a lie. Do you understand what a lie is?"

Gage nodded.

"The man will be in jail, locked up for a long time."

"Oh."

She smiled at her son's pure acceptance of right and wrong. "Since it's my last night off and I won't see you for a few days, how about if we go to McDonald's? We'll get you a Happy Meal with a toy, and you can make friends in the playground."

Gage gave her a big smile, lifted two fists, and gave a double thumbs-up.

7

———

PAYTON

Dazzle pulled into a gas station and got out, stretching his legs as he stood. "Take your sister to the bathroom. And "don't talk to anyone." He handed her a twenty-dollar bill. "Get yourself some snacks if you want."

After getting out of the SUV, she smiled at her boyfriend. "You're so good to us, Dazzle."

"You remember that, Candi."

"Candi?"

Dazzle grinned. "New life, new name. Your new name is Candi."

Brooke exited the vehicle. "Payton, I have to go to the bathroom."

She looked at her little sister. "Call me Candi. I have a new name now."

The younger girl frowned. "Huh?"

Dazzle rested his hand on Brooke's shoulder. "You're starting a new life, so you should get new names. I named your sister Candi because she's as sweet and smooth as a bar of white chocolate." He grinned at Brooke. "I've chosen Kitty for you because you're soft, innocent, and inquisitive."

"I don't want it. I like my own name just fine."

Dazzle frowned, grabbed Payton's arm, and tugged her to the back of the SUV. "You'd better get your sister on board, Candi. I only brought her along because you insisted. I can't have her wasting my time if she isn't going to be a good girl. I'll leave her right here—I mean it."

Payton ran her hand from Dazzle's shoulder to his elbow. "Don't worry. I'll take care of it. Let me take her to the bathroom, and I'll explain it all to her. She's just a little girl. Don't worry. She'll listen to me."

"She'd better, or I don't think I can take you either—no matter how much I love you and want us to be together."

Payton blinked back tears. "I promise. She'll behave."

Dazzle kissed her on the cheek. "I knew I could count on you." He turned away and removed the nozzle from the pump.

Payton sighed, wishing he'd kissed her on the lips, and took her sister's hand. "Come on. Let's use the restroom, and then I'll let you pick out your favorite snack."

Brooke was quiet until they got to the empty restroom. "I want to go home. I miss Mom and Dad and, they're probably worried about us. And I don't want to be called Kitty. My name is Brooke."

"Listen, Dazzle freed us from Mom and Dad ruling our lives. Look at the adventure we're on right now. The furthest we've ever been away from home was Salt Lake City, and now we're heading to Nevada." She grabbed her sister's hands and squeezed them. "Las Vegas is also called Sin City. How cool is that?"

Brooke pulled her hands away, went into a stall, and locked the door. "I don't want to go to a city that sins. I only went with you to meet Dazzle and make sure he wasn't some murdering weirdo. Mom and Dad would never approve of us going to Las Vegas. It goes against everything we've been taught."

Payton went into another stall. "What if I get Dazzle to let me use my cell phone and call them? You can talk to them and tell them we're okay."

They exited their stalls at the same time and went to the sink to wash their hands.

"You *know* they're going to tell us to come home. I don't think your boyfriend is going to let us use your phone."

Payton wadded the paper towel she'd used to dry her hands and tossed it into the trash can before grabbing her little sister's bicep and squeezing it tight. "Brooke, I'm sick of all the rules! Between Mom, Dad, and the church…they never let us go out and do anything fun. And if we *do* go somewhere, we always have to go with someone from church." She smiled. "Dazzle is the best thing that's ever happened in my life. We're in love and he's going to marry me." She turned the little girl's body to face her so she could look into her eyes. "I'm not going to let you screw this up for me. I promise we'll always stay together and that I'll take really good care of you. But if Dazzle wants to give you a new name, you need to take it and be glad about it." She loosened her grip on her sister's arm. "Do you think you can do that…for me?"

Brooke looked at her with wide eyes. "Will you promise me that if I don't like it with Dazzle, that we'll both go home?"

"I love him, and we're going to have a big house in the Hollywood Hills. I can't promise that I'll ever want to go back. But if you want to go home, I'll make sure that Dazzle puts you on a plane right back to Boise—right back to Mom and Dad."

8

ROSA

osa Juarez had worked as a housekeeper for Robyn McGee for five years. The work was easy because Miss Robyn was a tidy person who picked up after herself. It was the only reason she'd taken the job. It was good, easy money, especially when compared to her full-time job with a famous game-show host who wasn't all that funny—or nice off stage. He also had a foul-mouthed slob of a wife who stacked every dirty dish she could in the kitchen on Rosa's days off.

As she walked to the bus, Rosa wondered how having a child in Miss Robyn's house would change things.

Her employer's announcement had shocked her. It had been the first Rosa had heard of her even wanting a child.

In spite of the Botox injections and the hours she spent in her home gym, the casting director wasn't getting any younger. It surprised Rosa that, in her forties, Miss Robyn wanted the responsibility of a little boy.

Preparing the boy's room had thrown Rosa's schedule off. She'd hurried through her other tasks, even cutting a few corners, to make it to the bus stop at her usual time.

The June evening was uncomfortably warm. She took a seat on the slatted bench in the ivy-covered shelter and wiped her brow.

The other housekeepers greeted her warmly and chatted while waiting for their ride.

From her years working in Bel Air, Rosa knew there was a hierarchy, even among the domestic help. Angelica was the queen bee. She worked for a power couple who were riding high in feature films. The pair lived next door to Miss Robyn and were a regular feature in the gossip magazines that blasted scandalous affairs and subsequent blow outs. Angelica loved dishing details about what was really happening in that house, which wasn't nearly as exciting as the magazines proclaimed.

Then, there was Sophia, who worked for a teen heart-throb singer. She advised the singer was sullen, but nice to her. His parents were a different story. The mother bossed the help around, and the man regularly got handsy with her. Sophia rolled her eyes and shook her head.

Angelica looked at Rosa. "What is happening with your lady?"

She shrugged. "Not much. Just the same old thing." Rosa didn't like to gossip about her clients. She learned early on you couldn't trust anyone in Los Angeles—even people you thought were friends.

9

———

ROY

Considering Friday was one of his regularly scheduled days off, Roy had an unusual amount of work-related duties—tasks he hadn't planned for on the day he usually earmarked for a fun activity with Gage.

He had tried not to let it ruin his mood, but he'd been ticked off since receiving a phone call from Lacey Galloway. He'd first met the sergeant during the Internal Affairs investigation into the sex scandal and subsequent death of his former boss, Glen Haywood. At the time, his marriage to Amber had been in tatters, but even during those depressing times, he'd recognized the sergeant's straightforward manner and her ability to see through BS.

She was a straight-shooter, and he liked her.

Lacey called this morning wanting to go over his testimony in the trial of Justin Lowe. The disabled former cop faced rape and homicide charges connected to the Haywood case.

The intrusion into his family time was frustrating but he was pleased she'd contacted him.

Roy wanted to review the case over the phone, but Lacey wasn't having it. As a compromise, she offered to pick him up and take him to brunch.

He had to pick up his son, so he suggested she meet him at his apartment, they'd pick up Gage, and then they could grab a bite. With his divorce in the works, his social life was lacking. Of course, prepping for trial testimony wasn't a date, but it was female interaction—something he hadn't explored in quite a while.

He had a few minutes to tidy up his apartment before he heard a knock on the door. His nervousness annoyed him. *Good God, you're a grown man, not a horny teenager.* He opened the door.

Lacey stood in a navy pantsuit with a smile on her face. "I was thinking on the way over that maybe we could go over your testimony here…*before* you get your son. I'm not sure that what we'll be discussing is appropriate for your son's ears."

He nodded. "Yeah, I thought of that, but Amber is working watch three and she tries to get in a long nap before she goes in."

Lacey made a face. "6:00 pm to 6:00 am. I hated that shift."

He nodded. "Me too, but Amber loves it." He grabbed his keys and phone from a small table near the door. "Gage can watch videos on my phone while we talk. He won't hear a thing we're saying." He'd walked the sergeant to his pickup truck in the resident parking lot and opened her door.

She grinned as she slid into the passenger seat. "Very gallant. Not what I'm used to from other cops."

He felt his face warm. It was true. In the cop world, male and female officers treated each other as equals. No male cop in his right mind would treat a female cop in such a traditional manner. She might interpret his actions as though he thought she was fragile or incapable.

He settled himself into the driver's seat. "Sorry. Away from the work, my manners are pretty ingrained."

She laughed. "It just means you were raised well. Don't get me wrong. It's nice to occasionally be treated as a woman. I just don't expect it from a cop."

He grinned. "I'll try to rein in my chivalry."

Twenty minutes later, he pulled into the driveway of the home he and Amber had once shared.

"Nice house," Lacey said.

He made a wry face and sighed. "Yeah. It was the least I could do after my, uh…bad behavior." As an integral part of the Lowe investigation, Lacey was well aware of the case where Roy had slept with his female partner. He put on the parking brake. "I'll be right back." As he strode up the front walkway, the front door to the house opened.

Amber, dressed in her black yoga pants and mint-green tank top, opened the door wider as he approached.

She's so damn pretty. He stepped into the foyer and looked around for his son. "Where's Gage?"

Tension emanated from his wife's features as she looked

at his truck in the driveway. "He forgot his teddy. He ran back to get it." Her tone was clipped and flat.

He cocked his head. "Are you okay?"

"I'm fine," she said, pressing her lips into a thin line.

He turned away as he felt his lips twitching into the shape of a small smile. Amber's moods were no longer his concern. Maybe divorce wasn't the disaster he'd feared.

Gage came running into the foyer.

At the sight of her son, Amber's features relaxed. "You have a good time at Daddy's house. Be a good boy and don't eat too much junk food."

The toddler nodded.

"Give mommy a hug," Roy said.

Gage held his arms up to Amber.

She didn't disappoint and lifted the child, smothering him with kisses.

"Just so, we're on the same page," he said, "you'll pick Gage up on your way home from work Monday morning and take him to school."

"Tell me again why I'm doing that? You usually take him to school on Mondays."

"The Justin Lowe trial starts on Monday. I need to look over my notes, meet with the DA, and prep."

"Oh yeah," she said. "I got subpoenaed too, but I'm on call."

He remembered Lacey was in the car and grabbed his son's backpack. "Well, I've got to go. Come on, Gage. Let's go get some lunch."

Amber's features hardened again as she opened the front door. "Bye."

Roy held Gage's hand as they walked toward the car. "Hey, buddy, I have a friend I want you to meet."

10

———

BROOKE

Brooke tried not to stare as Dazzle drove them into Las Vegas.

"This is Las Vegas Boulevard, better known as the strip." He nodded at two tall copper-colored curved towers. "That's the Wynn and Encore. It's where a lot of whales come to stay."

"Whales? They have rooms for whales?"

Dazzle looked in the rearview mirror at her and grinned. "No, Kitty. Here, in Las Vegas, a whale is a person who has lots of money to spend on gambling and other exciting…recreation."

Payton pointed across the street. "Is that a pirate ship?"

"Yes. And that hotel right there has a volcano that erupts every hour."

Payton giggled. "I've never seen anything like this."

"Wait until you see the Bellagio. They've got huge fountains that dance to music."

Brooke couldn't believe their luck as they drove past the fountains. and the water was actually dancing. The swaying jet streams bounced and moved perfectly to the music.

"Dazzle, do you think we could stay there?" Payton's voice sounded just like it did when she was trying to talk Mom and Dad into getting her way.

He scoffed. "Damn, girl. I don't have money for that place—at least not right now." He turned and headed south. "I want you to meet the rest of the family."

"Your parents live here in Las Vegas?"

Dazzle took his eyes off the road to look at her sister. "Hell no. Do I look like a man that still lives with his mommy and daddy?"

"Well, then who are we going to meet?"

"You'll see when we get there."

Brooke didn't understand her sister's fascination. She didn't like Dazzle and hoped Payton would come to her senses soon.

Once they turned off the strip, the scenery changed. Nothing looked lush, glitzy, or shiny. Instead, the streets were dirty, trash-filled, and depressing. The further they drove the worse their surroundings.

Although her heart was pounding, Brooke found her voice. "Are we still in Las Vegas?"

He grinned in the mirror. "Of course we are. Why do you ask?"

"It's not pretty like where the big hotels were."

He shrugged. "The strip is for tourists. They keep it clean and polished so people will spend their money in the casinos and hotels." He turned down another street, then pulled to the side of the road as an ambulance sped by with its siren blaring.

Once the emergency vehicle passed, he continued down the road.

Minutes later, he turned into the lot of a dingy motel. "Here we are. This is our motel for tonight. We'll get up early and head to LA…and home." He found an empty spot between a couple of old battered cars littering the parking lot, and turned the engine off. "Get your stuff and follow me."

PART II

11

———

ROBYN

Robyn looked out her kitchen window at the stacked rock water feature in her backyard. Surely Logan wouldn't take to climbing the sculpture, or worse yet, be interested in the pool. She pushed away the thoughts that she really didn't know much about children.

She'd been an only child, and because her movie-producer parents were always working, there'd been a revolving door of caregivers in her home. She hadn't understood why until, at the age of eleven, she'd stumbled upon her father and her nanny doing "it" on the couch in his home office. They hadn't realized they had an audience, so she'd watched, mesmerized by their guttural noises and frenzied coupling.

When she'd told her mother what she'd seen, her mom

had sighed. "Why are you telling me this, Robyn? Now I've got to find *another* nanny for you."

"Don't you care?"

"Well, I don't like it, but that's what men do. You'll learn that soon enough."

"But you're *married*."

"A marriage certificate is just a piece of paper. If you can find a man who doesn't screw around on his wife, you'd better keep him. Personally, I don't know any man who could keep his pecker in his pants."

Robyn was thirteen when she learned her mother was screwing most of the male leads in the movies she and her husband produced.

As she grew older, Robyn saw the male species as a challenge. Could *she* attract married men and get them to break their wedding vows and have sex with her?

Turned out, it wasn't hard at all, but after a failed marriage, and now in her early forties, she finally found a married man that she couldn't tempt to cheat. She wanted him, but one question remained.

How do I get him?

12

AMBER

Amber sat on the passenger side of the black-and-white and entered the disposition of the last call she and her partner had handled into their car computer.

"With the Fourth of July coming, we're going to be handling a lot more of these fireworks calls," Ed Waller said.

Amber finished her entry and sighed. "These calls are a big waste of time. The suspects are usually long gone, and if they're not, you and I give them a warning and send them on their way."

Her partner smiled. "Before the big budget cuts, there used to be task forces of officers and firefighters whose main function was locating big caches of illegal fireworks. They were successful too."

"Yeah, that was then, and this is now. Do more with less."

Her partner shot her a look. "What's up with you? You're not usually such a Debbie Downer."

"I'm just tired. I didn't sleep well."

Ed pulled their car out into traffic. "First day back is always tough. One thing about working overnight is that your sleep schedule is bound to be screwed up."

"Roy came to pick up Gage this morning. He had a woman in the car."

"Ooooh, that explains a lot." Ed chuckled.

"What's that supposed to mean?"

"How long have you guys been separated?"

"About a year and a half."

"This the first time you've seen him with another woman?"

"Yeah. So what?"

Her partner's tone softened. "It must have hurt."

She turned, looking out the window, and blinked back building tears. "A little."

"Have you dated anyone since you guys split?"

Amber recalled her short-lived romance with one of her previous training officers. "One guy. It didn't last long."

"So, didn't you think Roy would do the same thing? Eighteen months is a long time."

"Yeah." She squirmed in her seat. "But I didn't expose our son to my…friend. Roy's squeeze was in his car, sitting in *my* driveway, and spending the afternoon with *my* son."

"Well, partner, I guess what you have to decide is if you're upset that your husband is dating another woman or that he's introducing his new piece to your son."

"I'm upset about all of it. I don't like another woman in the picture at all."

Ed made a face. "Well, maybe you need to get that figured out."

13

———

DAZZLE

Dazzle's afternoon had been rough. Sugar had eyed the new girls with jealousy, only made worse when he'd gotten a separate room for him and the newcomers, leaving the other three girls in the same room they'd been sharing while he'd been gone.

Sugar came to his room at his request. He needed to collect the money earned while he was gone, so he sent Candi and Kitty to meet the other girls.

As they walked out of the room, the two unsophisticated sisters tried not to stare at Sugar in her Daisy Duke shorts, blue tube top, and thigh-high boots, but failed miserably.

Once they were gone, Sugar started. "I don't know why *I* can't stay in your room with you. The new girls can stay with Diamond and Eden."

"Because neither of them are seasoned. I'll take care of that tonight while you and the other girls are out working."

"I'll show them the ropes. You always say I'm your best girl."

"You need to remember who takes care of you. Just do what I say. I don't want to take a hand to you, but I will."

"Okay, Daz. I'm sorry."

"Where's the money from the last few days?"

She reached into her top and pulled out two wads of rolled up bills and handed them to him.

He unrolled the money, put the stacks together, and splayed them out like a gigantic poker hand. "Shit. Three girls, working in Vegas for four days, and you barely made three thou?" He grabbed her arm and yanked her close. "Where's the rest of it? You sure Diamond and Eden didn't hold out on you?"

"There ain't no more. I promise. We slowed our roll 'cause we were afraid of gettin' busted by vice cops."

He let go of her arm.

She glared at him. "If we got picked up, you weren't here to bail us out."

He backhanded her. "Then you'd sit your fat ass in jail until I did come for you."

The girl bowed her head.

He wrapped his arms around her and smoothed her hair. "I'm sorry, Sugar. When you girls don't make your quota, I get frustrated. I'm trying to save as much money as I can so you and I can get that house in the Hollywood Hills above the Sunset Strip. Then we'll give up the game, retire, and live the highlife doing whatever we want."

"Oh, Daz, I want that more than anything. I'll tell the girls, for the next week, our quota is increased by fifty bucks a night."

He grinned. "That is why I love you best." He swatted her ass." Now, you and those other lazy hos get to work—you all slacked off while I was gone. If you get heat from any of the local girls or their daddy's, text me."

"Don't worry. I know how to handle myself."

He smiled at Sugar. "That's why you're my main girl." With the sun setting, Dazzle was anxious to get Sugar, Diamond, and Eden out on the streets. "Now get a move on and bring Daddy home some big bucks." Once the other girls were out working, he went to get Candi. "Kitty, I want you to stay in this room for a while. Candi and I have some things to discuss."

He took gratification in the younger girl's panicked face.

"Why can't I go too?"

He leveled his gaze into hers. "Because I said so." He nodded toward the TV. "You can watch whatever you want on the TV. In fact, how about I rent you a movie that I *know* your parents would never let you watch."

The kid's frightened expression was replaced with confusion.

He reconsidered. "Maybe you're not ready for that. You can watch whatever you want, just don't come out of this room, and don't talk to anyone. If someone comes to the door, don't answer it. We'll be in room 216."

"Payton, please don't leave me. I'm scared."

Dazzle strode toward the crying Kitty and slapped her across the face. "Shut up. And her name is Candi!"

Kitty put her hand to her face and sobbed.

"You'll be fine here. I'll come and get you later and you can sleep with us." He grabbed Candi's arm and dragged her from the room.

14

ROY

Roy sat in bed, reviewing the reports on the three missing boys from Valley Bureau. Unfortunately, his mind kept wandering back to his time spent with Lacey Galloway.

He hadn't known how she'd react to Gage, because she'd mentioned she hadn't been around kids much. But had she not disclosed her history, he'd have never known. She'd engaged his son in conversation about the latest dinosaur toys and hottest video games for toddlers.

At first, Gage had been shy, but he'd warmed quickly.

At the restaurant, they hadn't discussed the upcoming Lowe trial—the place had been too noisy. He'd suggested they go back to his apartment where Gage could take a nap and then they could go over his testimony.

Everything had gone smoothly—so much so that as he'd

walked the Internal Affairs sergeant to the door, he'd asked her if she'd like to go to dinner sometime.

"I'd like that," she'd replied, and handed him one of her business cards with her personal cell number written on the back. "Call me," she'd said as sauntered out of his apartment.

He set aside the reports and grabbed his phone.

After a quick search of restaurants, settling on one in Santa Monica on the beach, he was about to call her until he saw it was after midnight.

With a heavy sigh, he returned his attention to the missing juvenile reports. The first, a four-year-old boy, happened about three weeks ago when he vanished from the front yard at his grandparents' home. They were watching the child while the parents were on vacation. The boy was playing in the front yard, and the grandfather went inside to use the bathroom. There was no video at the grandparents' house, but a neighbor's camera had caught a light-colored van driving slowly down the road.

Unfortunately, there was only one camera on the street and no way to know if the vehicle was involved. The boy was still out there, somewhere.

The second case was just as baffling. A two-year-old boy disappeared from a church carnival. One minute the toddler was watching his older brother throw rings around glass bottles, the next minute…he was gone. There were two witnesses who said they thought a Hispanic girl had led the boy away, but the witnesses were kids themselves, aged ten and twelve.

The two-year-old had been missing for two weeks.

The last boy was abducted ten days ago from a park

near his home where he was playing with friends. A skinny white girl, in her teens, was spotted asking the young boys to help her find her puppy. Most of the boys ignored the request, but eight-year-old Martell agreed to help.

The boy's friends said the girl led Martell to the other side of the park.

One boy said he saw a white van parked at the curb and that the side door was open.

The detectives handling Martell's case had a sketch done of the girl who said she'd lost her puppy. Unfortunately, the rendering was vague. Martell's case was in the news for about three days but was then replaced by the discovery of the body of a B-list actor in the Hollywood Hills.

Roy sighed and rubbed his hands across his face. Three boys gone within three weeks' time. Most of the sex offenders living near the locations where the boys were last seen had already been interviewed by detectives. But that didn't mean they couldn't return and make a surprise compliance check.

The media may have forgotten Martell, but Roy would not.

15

———

PAYTON

As Dazzle pulled her out of the room where Brooke sat crying, Payton could barely walk. She was stunned. *I have to say something. What should I say?*

He unlocked the door to their room and pushed her inside.

"Dazzle, I don't think you should have hit Br—Kitty. She's just a little girl. And she's scared."

He locked the deadbolt and then turned to her. "Who the hell do you think you are to tell me what to do?" He strode toward her.

She held up her hands. "Wait. I'm sorry. It's just...our parents never even spanked us. This is all new. We're a little off balance."

A sinister grin formed on his face. "Yeah, well, you're

going to be learning a lot of new things. You and Kitty
both."

It was at that moment she realized she was in way over
her head. She wanted to go home, and just like her little
sister, she was scared.

"You stink." He bobbed his head toward the bathroom.
"Go take a shower."

She glanced at the other room, wondering if there was a
window. She'd get Brooke and run away. She'd call their
parents. She started toward the bathroom.

"Wait. I'm feeling like a shower, too. We'll take one
together."

Her mouth dropped open as her cheeks warmed. She
shook her head. "Oh, I-I-I don't think, um, I mean, uh, I
don't think I'm ready for anything like that."

The maniacal grin returned. "There you go thinking
again. Now that you're with me, you don't have to think. I'll
do it for you. All you have to worry about is doing what I
say." He dropped the evil smile and his eyes narrowed. "Get
in the bathroom, take off your clothes, and start the shower.
I'll be right there."

If she thought she was scared before, she was terrified
now. *What do I do? Maybe bang on the walls and yell for help?*

"Move!"

She shuffled toward the bathroom. Out of the corner of
her eye, she saw him pick up his phone.

As she stepped inside the tiny room, she considered
locking him out of the bathroom, but the lock was pretty
flimsy. He'd have no problem breaking through the door. To
her dismay, there was no window, either. *Now what?* With
numb fingers, she fumbled with the shower knobs and

managed to remove her clothes. *Maybe if I take my shower fast, I can be done before he finishes his call.*

She was lathering herself with soap when he pulled the shower curtain open, and she saw a naked man for the first time.

He seemed calm as he climbed into the shower and stood next to her.

She averted her eyes from his lower torso and his repulsive erection.

"Hey, I'm sorry. I was short with you and rough with Kitty. I'm just tired." He dropped his gaze to his penis. "As you can see, I'm carrying a lot of tension." He placed his hands on her shoulders and ran them down her arms.

In spite of herself, she shivered.

He pulled her into a hug and began kissing her.

She wanted to concentrate on his kiss, but his penis pressing into her belly was distracting.

He pulled back. "Touch it," he whispered.

"I…I…don't want to. I don't know what to do."

Without a word, he placed her hand on his body.

Both intrigued and repulsed, she tried to focus on what he was having her do, but images of her parents and church leaders filled her mind. She was committing a sin. Right here. Right now. As disturbed as she was, a part of her was curious.

She moved her hands over his body and shifted her eyes to his face. She couldn't help but notice his reactions to her touch.

He started kissing her again.

After a few minutes, he pulled away from her again. "Come to the bed. Let me make love to you."

There was a strange feeling—fear, shame, and hesitancy, at first, but also an urgency in her lower stomach. *You're about to lose your virginity.* She imagined what would happen next… and realized how scared she was. *It's okay. You want to.*

They stepped out of the shower and toweled off.

He kissed her neck, her back, then led her to the bed.

Dazzle loves you. He was just tired, like he said. See how gentle he is and how good he makes you feel? This is why you left home. He loves you. Dazzle loves you. He wouldn't hurt you.

He showed her the many ways she could please him.

At first shy and timid, by the time he was spent, she felt so worldly, so grown-up, and so powerful.

Afterward, he fell asleep and snored in her ear. Afraid to move or disturb his sleep, she lay on her back, looking at the ceiling and thinking about how much her life had changed in the last twenty-four hours. *You're with a man who will love you and take care of you—and you love him!* She pushed away her earlier thoughts of fear and the mental images of her parents and how worried they must be. Eventually, she drifted off to sleep too.

A knock on the motel room door had her sitting up, clutching the sheet to her chest.

Dazzle groaned and rolled off the bed.

She gasped when he opened the nightstand drawer and pulled out a gun.

"Shhh, be quiet." He shuffled to the door, snagging his shorts off the floor as he went, and looked through the peep-hole. "Just a sec." He pulled the shorts on.

She didn't know if she should run to the bathroom, get dressed, or what.

He unlocked the door and opened it wide, and three

men snaked into the room, their eyes focused on her and the sheet held over her breasts.

"Candi, I want you to meet some of my associates." He smiled. "I asked them to come over and help make your stay here in Vegas memorable."

16

AMBER

At 2:30 am, Amber and Ed finished a traffic stop involving a man for driving without his vehicle headlights on—a common practice for someone who'd had too much to drink.

Given that the bars had just closed, they thought for sure they'd be making an arrest for drunk driving. Instead, they'd discovered a bleary-eyed plastic surgeon fresh from four hours of surgery stitching together the face of a sixteen-year-old girl. She'd gone through a car windshield—an accident caused by her drunk boyfriend.

"I'm really sorry, officers. I'm dead tired. I just wasn't thinking straight."

After checking that the doctor's driver's license was valid and he didn't have any warrants, they sent him on his way with a warning to get some rest.

Ed slid into the passenger seat of their patrol car. "How about we go back to the station for Code 7?"

She smiled. "Great minds think alike. What did Anna pack for you tonight?"

"Leftover meatloaf, mashed potatoes, and carrots."

"Sounds delicious. I've got a salad with grilled chicken breast. Not fancy, but healthy."

Ed sighed. "I hate that it isn't safe for us to eat out for lunch. Even if our choices are limited to the only two places open all night; the pancake diner or the twenty-four-hour Mexican joint. Then again, the last thing I want to do is eat a sandwich or burrito covered in *secret sauce* they use just for cops."

A short time later, they were in the deserted lunchroom at Foothill station.

Amber swallowed a bite of lettuce and chicken. "I wish I knew how I really felt about Roy." She sighed.

"You know," Ed said, "Anna and I were married for about four years when we split up for a few months."

Amber gasped. "What? I had no idea. You two look like the perfect pair."

Ed flashed a wry smile. "Yeah, don't believe everything you see. I was all about work and being a hard charger. I made lots of arrests which resulted in lots of overtime and court time. I was never home."

"Did she cheat on you?"

Ed looked horrified. "Oh, no! Nothing like that. Although, I'm not sure I would have blamed her. We had two kids by then, and she was running the household pretty much by herself." He sipped from his soda. "I was working nights, and after our shift, my buddies and I would go have a few at the Sip and Savor. Sometimes, I'd come home at dawn hammered.

"Did you cheat on her?"

He shook his head. "No…but I came close." He shifted in his chair. "Anna couldn't take it anymore, so she packed up the kids and left. I hit rock bottom then. All the things I was already doing I increased about tenfold."

"Did you date while you were separated?"

"I went out with a couple of gals, and yeah, I slept with them." He shrugged. "But the truth was…I knew I'd screwed up. I missed my family, and I wanted them back."

"How did Anna get over the fact you'd slept with other women?"

"She didn't ask, and I didn't tell." He smiled when she stared at him, wide-eyed and with her mouth open. "I didn't ask her either…and she didn't tell."

Amber shook her head. "That's the thing. Roy and I weren't separated. He flat out cheated on me."

"And it cost him his wife and son. Maybe he's hit rock bottom. Maybe you ought to give him another chance. I know Anna and I are grateful for each day we've spent putting our lives back together. Maybe you can, too."

17

PAYTON

Payton winced as she awoke in the dreary motel room. She stared at the bright sunlight seeping through the vertical slats of the cheap blinds.

Everything hurt. Then, in a rush, she remembered why. Bile rose in her throat. She clamped her lips together and swallowed hard, willing herself not to be sick…at least until she made it to the bathroom.

Forced to dash to the bathroom through excruciating pain in her limbs and insides, she barely made it to the bathroom before her stomach emptied.

She collapsed to the floor and rested her head on the toilet seat—something she never would have done two days ago. *What have I done?* This never would have happened if she'd stayed in Boise. *How could I be so stupid?* She was hurting, broken, and afraid.

Dazzle shuffled into the bathroom doorway. He was naked. "Flush the toilet and get out of the way. I need to pee."

"I can't. I'm too sick and sore." It scared her how frail her voice sounded.

"I *said,* get out of the way."

She tried to look at him. Her skull felt like someone had lodged an axe between her eyes, and her vision was blurry. "Dazzle, I'm sorry, I can't. I just hurt so bad."

He took two steps, grabbed her arm, and dragged her to the bedroom, where he dropped her to the floor.

"Ohhhh," she moaned, as she heard the toilet flush, and then the sound of him peeing. She had bruises from her shoulder to her elbow.

Dazzle hadn't done that. It had been his friends as she'd tried to fight them off. They'd all taken turns with her. Some of them more than once.

She rolled to her side and pushed into a sitting position, gasping at the pain in her ribs. Looking at her legs, there was more bruising on her upper thighs.

She see-sawed her jaw, left then right, as memories of the night before caused her stomach to lurch again.

"I've got some pills for you. They'll take away most of the pain," Dazzle said, stepping out of the bathroom and scratching himself.

She shook her head. "No. I don't want any drugs."

"Do I look like someone who cares what you want? You'll do as I say. We gotta get back to LA. We're leaving in a half-hour, so get your ass in gear. We gotta get back to LA." He thrust out his hand with two pills in it. In the other, he had a bottle of vodka. "Take 'em."

She almost choked as the alcohol burned its way down her throat.

"Dazzle, I think maybe Brooke and I should go home. If I could just call my parents, I'm sure they'll come for us."

He laughed. "Candi, face facts. After last night, your family doesn't want you. You're nothin' but a turned-out whore. From now on, you don't make *any* decisions. I own you—you *and* your sister—and you'll do as I say. Both of you."

18

———

ROY

Roy slept until Gage shuffled into his room and tapped him on the arm.

"Daddy…Paw Patol."

He lifted the little boy into his bed and turned on the bedroom television to his son's favorite animated show. There was nothing he liked better than Saturdays with his son.

When the show was over, Roy carried his boy from the bed and into the kitchen. "What's it going to be today, champ? Pancakes? French Toast? Scrambled eggs?

"Pancakes!"

"What kind? Blueberry or strawberry?"

"Chocit chip!"

"Chocolate chips are for cookies, not breakfast."

"Mama makes chocit-chip pansakes," Gage said, nodding.

"Well, then that makes it okay for sure," Roy said, laughing while pulling out a large bowl and whisk.

After food and cleaning up, they hit the grocery store. Gage was like a beacon, attracting the attention of women of all ages, shapes, and sizes—and that gave Roy an idea.

As they put the groceries away, Roy asked Gage if he wanted to go to a park and play.

"Yay," the little boy said, while clapping his hands.

Roy drove to the same park where the most recent missing boy, Martell, was last seen.

He parked, got his son out of the truck, and they headed to the playground.

"Higher!" Gage squealed from the swings as Roy's attention was focused on a shapely blonde jogging past the tot lot.

Just beyond the blonde, a white van pulled to the curb.

The passenger door opened.

Roy's heart raced, waiting for someone to come out. *Please be a skinny white girl.*

Unfortunately, it was a buxom brunette who exited the van. She opened the door and four kids jumped out, yelling as they tore across the grass toward the playground.

Roy stopped pushing Gage when his phone rang. Caller ID showed Van Nuys W/C. "Buckner."

"This is Lieutenant Ramona Enloe, Van Nuys. I think we may have found the two-year-old boy that's been missing for the past few weeks."

"Where'd you find him?"

"A patrol unit stopped a white van for blowing a red

light at Vanowen and Woodman. The kid was strapped in the front passenger seat."

"Does he seem okay? Are you sure it's him?"

"Hard to say. He's so little. But he doesn't seem to have any physical injuries that we can see."

"Who was driving the van?"

"A parolee who's done time for burglary, GTA, and assault."

"What does he say about the kid?"

"He said the boy belongs to his girlfriend. He hasn't seen her for two days and only knows the girlfriend's first name —Sarah."

"Swell." Roy ran a hand through his hair. "At least we've got the boy. I'll notify the D-3 at Valley Bureau Sex Crimes. You'll need to notify your Sex Crimes detectives and get the kid checked out at the hospital."

"Yeah, I've already got those folks rolling."

"Excellent. Have your Sex Crimes guys give me a call when they've got more."

"You got it."

"Hey, lieutenant?"

"Yeah?"

"Find out what those patrol coppers like to drink."

There was a chuckle on the line. "Will do."

19

———————

ROBYN

Robyn sat on her patio, by the pool sipping on a glass of Chardonnay and listening to the second actor she'd hired on her recently purchased prepaid phone pressed to her ear.

"We got this. I promise! I confirmed the location and time changes, and we'll be there. We won't let you down."

"I'll text you when it's time. You've got to nail the scene in one take, Max. And no matter what happens, do not break character."

"Yes, Miss Heath. We both understand. And we'll receive a copy of the video for our portfolios, correct?"

"Absolutely."

"Will you be at the filming?"

"No, I'm afraid I have other commitments. I'll contact you later in the week with the video." She disconnected her call with Max, she pulled out her map, and went over her plans and timeline one more time for Monday.

She took another sip of her wine and made her way toward the bedroom she'd set up for her soon-to-be-son, Logan.

Gazing at the wonderland she'd built for him, she whispered, "If you can pull this off, Robyn, you can do anything."

20

DAZZLE

Dazzle needed speed. His days were too long and his nights endless…even the strongest energy drinks had no effect. The trip back to Los Angeles with his girls had him worn down to the point of barely functioning.

After they'd gotten through the checkpoint to re-enter California, he'd pulled over and told Sugar to drive his Escalade. At a pit stop in Baker, he'd watched Candi leaning against the window of the third-row seat, her eyes closed, while Kitty rubbed her sister's arms, whispering to her.

Dazzle wasn't sure making the trip to Boise was worth the hassle.

Sure, the pimp pipeline talked about how easy it was to get Midwest girls. Salt Lake City pimps made regular trips to Boise, Twin Falls, and even up north to Rexburg to find new girls. Eager to get a taste of life's wild side, the girls were easily duped into going off with a charismatic stranger.

Other teens were new out-of-staters who, along with their parents, had fled the dirty and dangerous streets of San Francisco, Los Angeles, and Portland to come to idyllic Idaho, Utah, or where evil wasn't supposed to prey. They let their guard down and didn't realize their mistake until it was too late.

But to Dazzle's way of thinking, traveling was a lot of work to get a commodity he could get easily at home. And, he hadn't even tapped the actual gold of this trip—Kitty.

Thankful for the shuteye while Sugar drove them home, he decided to drop a little something as soon as they got back to LA. Other than weed, he usually

avoided drugs, but the past week had kicked his ass.

He'd also have to teach Candi to smoke crystal meth before she hit the streets. She looked like crap after her turn-out in Vegas. Not only would the drug liven her up, but she'd drop her inhibitions as well. A win-win. 'Cause when the johns were happy, they came back for more.

As he drifted off to sleep, he thought about the 411 he picked up from the Vegas pimps. The hos were great for a low-end steady income, but the *real* money to be made was with little kids and babies. They said if you had a child— boy or girl—under the age of eight, you could command big bucks for filming them having sex and then sell videos on the dark web. But they also warned a ton of headaches came with kids that age. They said they used 'em quick and got out even quicker.

"Film the kids their first few times, then sell them to the highest bidder," was how one guy put it.

Dazzle was impressed. The Vegas guys drove a three-hundred-thousand Rolls Royce, which made him feel like nothin' in his SUV. He damn sure wanted to fatten up his bankroll, but he wasn't interested in the headaches of taking care of or housing little kids. *S'okay, though.*

He had a plan…a better plan.

PART III

21

───────

PAYTON

Payton was so sore she could barely move when the black SUV pulled in and parked at a seedy motel on a busy street called San Fernando Road. Across the street, an electronic sign showed it was 9:12 pm, and 73 degrees.

"Home sweet home," Sugar said, as she pulled into a parking spot next to the motel's office.

Dazzle rubbed his hands over his face. "You bitches wait here. I'll be right back." He got out of the vehicle and shuffled into the office.

Diamond turned around to look at her and Brooke. "Try not to set anything on the ground. This place is a dump. My other daddy wouldn't stay anyplace that had cockroaches. Don't know why this daddy won't spend a few extra bucks for a nicer home."

After Dazzle returned, the group gathered their belongings and settled into their rooms.

An hour later, Sugar came to the room Payton and Brooke shared with Dazzle. "Daddy went to get supplies." She tossed some clothes at Payton, who was still groggy from whatever pain pills Dazzle had given her. "Put these on. I'll be back in a few minutes to do your hair and make-up. Daddy is taking you out tonight and wants to leave in about a half-hour."

She gasped. "Tell him, I'm sorry. I feel terrible. I can't go anywhere."

Sugar sighed. "Candi, you need to understand you're not in control of your life anymore. Dazzle tells you what to do, when to do it, and how much you should get paid for doing it. He wants you to go out and work, and he's told me to get you ready. If he gets back and you're not good to go, I get a beating, you get a beating, and probably your little sister will get one, too—and he'll make you go out and work anyway. Now, cut the whining and put on those clothes."

"Sugar, I won't do it. I can't."

The other girl reached into her bra and pulled out a business card. "I'm only giving you this because I can see a ton of beatings in my future when you don't get with the program." She handed over the card. "First chance you get, call the lady on this card. She can help you."

Payton glanced at the card. "Victims of the Street. There is a way out." She looked at Sugar. "I don't have any money."

Sugar rolled her eyes and pulled out her makeup bag out of her purse. "Go home, Candi." She retrieved a compact and used her manicured fingernail to pry the small makeup mirror from the lid. "Take this money. Call a cab or get a ride share. Go to the address on the card. Talk to the woman on the card, and have her call your parents." She pulled out a twenty-dollar bill from beneath glass and handed to her. "Take your sister and go home, and whatever you do, don't let Daddy find the card or the money. He'll beat us all."

"Yes, Payton, let's go home," Brooke said.

The look on her sister's face broke her heart.

"For now…" Sugar sighed and pointed at the pile of clothes on the bed, "…get movin'. I've got a quota and you're cutting into my time."

"What about me?"

Sugar looked at Brooke. "You'll probably stay in the room. Enjoy it while you can. He'll get you out there working soon enough."

"Working? I'm not old enough to get a job."

Sugar laughed. "Girl, before you know it, you'll be doing more *jobs* in a night than a straight thirty-year-old does in a week."

Although she was still in pain, the lingering fuzziness from the meds Dazzle had given her took enough of the edge off for Payton to pull on the black miniskirt, fishnet stockings, and pink sequined top the other girl had thrown at her.

"Wear those again." Sugar pointed to the boots Payton had worn the previous night, and then pulled her hair into a tight ponytail.

By the time Sugar finished her makeup, Brooke said she thought her sister looked like a clown.

Sugar pushed her toward the door.

"Wait a minute!" Payton walked toward her sister and whispered in her ear. "Find a way to stay away from Dazzle. I'm going to get us out of here." She kissed Brooke on the cheek and went out the door with Sugar.

As they stood outside the motel door, she searched the parking lot. "Where do we go now? Where's Dazzle?"

Sugar shot her a look. "Girl…you're a 'ho. You don't get to call him Dazzle no more. He's Daddy to you and all the rest of us."

Payton shook her head. "No. It's different with me. He's going to marry me, and we'll live in a mansion in the Hollywood Hills. He told me so."

Sugar frowned. "He just told you that to get you to go with him. I'm his bottom."

She cocked her head at Sugar.

"I'm his main girl—his second in command. He loves me more than any of you. And *you* won't be living in the hills above Sunset Strip. He promised that to *me* a long time ago."

Payton frowned and looked past Sugar as Dazzle's black SUV pulled into the pot-holed parking lot. "We'll just see about that." Unable to believe she was so wrong about everything, she strode toward her boyfriend. "Sugar says that you told her the two of you were going to get married and live in a mansion in the Hollywood Hills. What's up with that?"

Dazzle stopped. "What's up with that? Who the hell are you, questioning me like that?"

"I'm your girlfriend." She felt her cheeks warm. "You said you loved me and that we'd get married." She realized how ridiculous she sounded—she was fourteen—but she still hoped everything he'd told her in Boise might be true.

A funny grin filled his face. "You trust me that much?"

Nod, you idiot.

"You'll get your chance to prove it tonight. I've got something special for you to do."

Her stomach turned realizing the mistake she'd made and remembering the treatment by his friends in Vegas. Did he have friends for her to *entertain* in LA?

He must have read her thoughts. "No. Nothing like Vegas. I'm going to teach you basic whoring. But first, I've got a treat for you." He reached into his pocket, pulled out a tiny clear plastic bag, and waved it at her.

She knew it was some kind of drug.

"Oh, Daz—Daddy, I love you for thinking of me, but I'm still kind of groggy from the pain pills you gave me."

"You gotta trust me, Candi. You're gonna feel like a million bucks." His gaze shifted to Sugar pacing in front of his motel room and smoking a cigarette. "I'll be right back." He strode toward Sugar, gave her a hug, leaning in close as he talked for a minute, and then motioned toward the street.

"Get Diamond and Eden out there, too," he yelled over his shoulder as he made his way back to Payton. "Okay, let's go for a ride."

22

DAZZLE

Dazzle drove Candi to a park on Sunland Boulevard and taught her how to smoke meth. He gave her a glass pipe, showed her how to get the contents in the right part of the bowl, and told her to hold the pipe halfway down the stem so she wouldn't burn her fingers. He then directed her to roll it back and forth so the flame from a lighter would heat the bowl evenly.

She almost choked the first time she inhaled, but it seemed to get easier for her the more she smoked.

Suddenly, she threw back her head and laughed. "For the first time in my life, I feel alive!"

He grabbed her and kissed her hard.

To his surprise, she'd returned his kiss and was bold enough to run her hand up his thigh. In response, he unzipped his pants and pulled her head into his lap.

After he finished, he drove her to a tattoo shop—Pussycat Ink—where he took all his girls, and told her he wanted to give her a gift. A tattoo.

She pouted when he wouldn't let her get the dolphin she wanted on the back of her neck.

"I want your ink to be a surprise," he'd said.

The meth must have eased the pain of getting the tattoo because she didn't complain.

After the artist wiped the area clean, he handed her a mirror so she could see the black dollar sign inked into her skin.

"Oh, a dollar sign," she mumbled.

Dazzle moved behind her and nuzzled the side of her neck. "Don't you love it, baby? It tells the world how much I value you." He could tell she didn't like it, but he didn't care.

She gave him a fake smile. "Yeah. I love it."

The tattoo guy put a layer of antibacterial ointment and plastic wrap over her tattoo.

Dazzle paid the guy, and off they went.

As he drove through the streets of the San Fernando Valley, he told her she was going to learn how to work on a track.

A few minutes later, he'd pulled into an alley off of San Fernando Boulevard. "Okay, go out there and stroll on the sidewalk. When the guys pull up, go to the window and ask them if they're looking for a date."

She stared at him. "You want me to go on a date…with a stranger?"

He frowned. "Are you really that stupid? You're going to have sex with them." He rattled off the terms of what they'd ask for and how much she should charge. He explained how to avoid being picked up by the cops, but he also told her, "Don't worry—if you do get arrested, I'll come bail you out. Besides, they won't keep you anyway. Whoring is a misdemeanor, and the jails are too full. They'll give you a ticket to go to court. No one goes back, though. It's no big deal."

She slumped against the window. "I'm *your* girl. I thought you loved me. Why would you want me to have sex with other men?"

He smiled and pulled her into his arms. "Of course, I love you. Like I told you before, getting a house in the Hollywood Hills is expensive. We need lots of money. I can't do it all myself. I need your help. Aren't you willing to work for our future together?"

With his arms tight around her, she nodded.

"Good. Now, when you get a date, direct them down that side street, do your job, then have them bring them back to where they picked you up."

She'd nodded and started to get out of the car.

"Take that plastic wrap off your neck. It's not a good look."

23

———

ANTONIO

In the San Fernando Valley, Antonio Lima made another pass down San Fernando Road on the lookout for any new girls on the stroll.

Most of the hookers knew him by sight. With his job as a car salesman, he sometimes snuck out in a dealership car to cruise the streets. Driving a different ride, he could fool them and get them to the window to make his pitch for a second—or even a third time.

He spotted a newcomer near Van Nuys Boulevard. *Darn! She can't be more than fifteen.* He drove past, about ten yards, and pulled to the curb.

He watched her from his side mirror as she tottered closer in her thigh-high stiletto boots and miniskirt. Her long blonde curls bounced, keeping time with her breasts concealed under the pink sequined top she wore.

He rolled down the window as she approached.

She leaned down, and he reassessed her age at about thirteen, fourteen tops.

"Looking for a date?"

"Maybe."

"What do you want?"

"It depends."

The kid's gaze darted all over the place, and her movements were jerky.

Probably high on meth.

"I'm not supposed to stay too long at the car. Are you a police officer?"

He held his arm out. "Do these look like cop tattoos?"

She scanned his arm full of gang markings. "So, do you want a date?"

"How much for a blow job?"

"Thirty."

He let out a whistle. "That's pretty steep for these parts." *She can probably get that price because she doesn't look skanky yet… and she's so young.*

"That's the price."

"What's your name?"

"Candi."

He grinned. "Hop in, Candi."

As he pulled away from the curb, she pointed. "Turn right at the next corner."

He followed her instructions toward a dark street where she told him to pull beneath a massive shade tree that blocked out the bright streetlights.

He turned off the engine, and she shifted in her seat.

"Wait," he said. "I don't really want a blow job." Even

in the darkness, he saw a spark of fear ignited in her expression.

"Wh…what do you mean? What do you want?"

"I promise I'm not going to hurt you. I just want to talk."

"I think I'd better go," she said, reaching for the door handle.

He grabbed her left wrist, careful not to squeeze too tightly. "Please. I just want to talk. My name is Antonio, and my sister used to be in the life. She's created a new life for herself, and you can too."

Her body relaxed. "My friends told me about guys like you."

He released her wrist. "What kind of guy is that?"

"Savior guys. You know, someone who wants to save me. I don't need to be saved."

"I think you do. I know you don't want to be here… doing things to a bunch of older men." He gave her his most charming smile. "Think about it—you're out here, night after night, making hundreds of dollars. How much of that do you get to keep? Probably none, or very little."

Her gaze flicked to the door handle again.

He worried she'd bolt. "I swear, I'm not going to hurt you, and I'm not going to get you into trouble."

She hesitated.

"If you ever need a place to go, there's a place on Sepulveda Boulevard north of Plummer called Victims of the Street. They will keep you safe. My sister, the one who used to be out on the streets works there now." He pulled a business card out of his shirt pocket. "How many days are you working?"

She didn't say anything.

"I'd like to talk to you again sometime."

Silence ticked by slowly, until she said, "I don't know. This is my first night." Her voice sounded resigned and very low.

"Please let me help you." He kept his voice to a whisper, too. "How many girls in your stable?"

"Stable?"

"How many girls is your pimp running?"

"Sugar, Diamond, Eden, and me." She picked at a hangnail then looked at him again. "My sister is with me, but she isn't doing what I do."

"Why not?"

"She's too young, but…but I heard my boyfriend talking to some of his friends about younger kids."

"How about the other girls? Are they all as young as you?"

"You ask too many questions. And I'm eighteen. I have papers."

"I know you're not eighteen. Did your pim— your daddy get the ID for you?"

"Do you want the blow job or not? I've got to get back."

"I can help you."

"No, you can't. No one can."

24

PAYTON

An hour later, Payton twisted in the front passenger seat, looking at the alley she'd just run. Gasping for breath, she bit her lip, waiting for Dazzle to come back to his Escalade, and thought about her warm and comfortable home in Idaho. *Mom and Dad must be so worried.* She thought about her first trick…the car with the young man. She was relieved he'd been nice. He'd turned out to be a savior date.

She remembered, during the drive from Vegas to LA, she'd heard Diamond and Eden mocking the men who tried to talk them out of the life, calling them savior dates.

"Like anyone would want to marry me after I've been with hundreds of guys," Diamond had sneered.

Eden had scoffed. "Probably thousands. Our woo-hoos are probably too worn out to have normal sex now."

After she and Antonio had talked, she'd asked him to take her back to where he'd picked her up.

To her surprise, he'd pulled out forty bucks, along with a business card for some charity, and handed them to her.

"Hide the card," he'd said. "Your pimp will beat you if he finds it."

She didn't believe him, but dropped the card inside her high-heeled boot…just in case. *First night working for your future with Dazzle, and you get two business cards to get out of the business. Maybe it's a sign.* As she got out of his car, she regretted telling him so much.

She'd barely walked ten feet when a battered sedan had pulled to the curb.

The man inside was old, fat, and had greasy hair. He smelled as though he hadn't bathed in a week. He wanted a blow job.

You're doing this for Dazzle and your life together in Hollywood.

After her second trick, she'd texted Dazzle she was going into a restaurant to use the bathroom. Once there, she'd actually taken a mini-sponge bath to wash away the stink. She'd also used the small bottle of mouth wash Dazzle had given her.

When she'd come out of the cafe, Dazzle had been waiting at the curb.

Relieved he came for her, she started to climb into the vehicle.

"What the hell you doing? You're not done yet."

"Oh, I thoug—"

"I told you. I do all your thinking. When you pick up your next trick, direct him to the street two blocks down, have him pull into the driveway of the auto body shop on the right. Got it?"

"Why do you want me to go there?"

Dazzle leveled a steady gaze on her. "Just do it," he'd said and pulled from the curb.

A few minutes later, an older man in a green Ford SUV pulled up. The driver looked better than her previous date. He was older, for sure, but definitely cleaner.

She'd walked up to the window and waited. It had taken him a second realize he'd have to roll the window down. "Looking for a date?"

"I…um…I guess I am."

"What kind of date do you want?"

"I'm not sure."

Alarm bells went off in Payton's head.

Dazzle had told her the cops always tried to get the girls to name a price for sex. "Make *him* tell you what he wants and how much he'll pay," Dazzle had said.

"Well, I can't go with you unless I know what we're going to do."

The old man had looked nervous.

Could it be his first time?

"Maybe we could talk and figure it out," he suggested.

"Talk isn't cheap," she'd replied, congratulating herself for coming up with the perfect line.

"Okay, I understand."

She'd got into the Ford and directed him, just like Dazzle had told her.

After a few awkward minutes of small talk, the man asked her name. She'd screwed up and told him her real name.

The man had asked if he could hold her hand.

New as she was to working the streets, she realized nothing was going to happen at the rate he was moving. She removed her hand from his and placed it high on his thigh.

When he didn't react, and knowing that time was money, she moved her hand further north.

Before long, she was performing her second paid blow job of the night, when suddenly, there was a tap on the window.

The john had pushed upright, and Payton had, too.

She'd gasped, recognizing Dazzle. Wearing a black knit mask over his face and pointing a gun at her and her date, he'd ordered her out of the Ford and pointed down the alley. "Run!"

Terrified, she'd done as he'd said.

Now, sitting in his black SUV waiting for him, she wondered what in the world possessed him to interrupt her date with a gun.

25

———

AMBER

Amber maneuvered their patrol car out of Foothill Station, westbound onto Osborne Street. "Just three more hours, Ed, and you can go home and sleep."

Ed sighed. "It's a good thing you're driving. I don't think I could stay awake behind the wheel."

"What makes you think I can?"

He swung his head to the left and rested it against the seat. "Because you don't have three kids under the age of seven."

"I told you a long time ago how babies happen. It's not my fault you don't listen and keep your baby-maker in your pants."

Two tones from the radio indicated an incoming call. "16A23, 16A23, see the man, unknown trouble, northwest corner of Kelowna and San Fernando Road. Handle Code 2."

Ed keyed the mic. "16A23, roger. Is there any further?"

The dispatcher responded quickly, "16A23, negative. He said he was borrowing a phone, needed the police, and then disconnected. No answer on the call back."

"Roger, that." Ed slammed the mic in its holder.

"We need to be careful," Amber said. "These days, it could be an ambush."

"In that part of town, more than likely it's a business dispute between a working girl and her john."

Amber made a U-turn and headed for San Fernando Road, turning north as the light switched to yellow.

Ed brought up the comments of the call on their car computer, but there was no new information.

A few minutes later, they spotted an older man, probably in his mid-fifties, wearing a Hawaiian shirt and khaki pants. He stood beside a green Ford Explorer in the driveway of a darkened auto repair shop waving his hands frantically over his head.

Amber scoffed. "Geez, it's 3:00 am on a Sunday morning. Not much is moving out here. Does he really think we don't see him?" She pulled their vehicle to the curb two car lengths from the Explorer.

"Let's hope this is nothing more than a quick report," Ed said, while exiting the black-and-white.

Amber smiled as she approached the man. "Did you call us?"

"Yes. Yes, I did."

Ed stopped beside her. "How can we help you?"

The man's hands shook as he removed his bifocals and

used the bottom of his gaudy shirt to rub the lenses. "I don't know where to start." He looked anxiously at Amber.

She shrugged and smiled. "I don't know what happened here, so let's start with your name."

The man put his glasses back on. "Milburn, John Milburn."

Ed elbowed her. "See? I told you it involved a john."

Ignoring him, Amber pulled a field interview card from her pocket. "Do you have your driver's license, sir?"

The man shook his head. "No. No. That's part of the problem. The man with the gun took my wallet, my phone, and even my car keys."

"Man with a gun? What man?" Ed placed a hand on the grip of his gun while his gaze surveyed the shadows. "Where'd he go?"

The older man waved his hand. "He's long gone. Ran down that alley, and I heard a car start and take off."

Amber held her pencil poised over her FI. "How long ago did this happen? Can you describe the man?"

Milburn shook his head and sighed. "It all started when I met a young lady outside the Kagel Street Kitchen. She asked me for a ride."

Amber shifted her stance. "A ride where?"

"She didn't say exactly. Just up the street."

"And you gave her a ride?"

"Yes. Yes, I did."

Amber exchanged glances with Ed. "Then what happened?"

"Well, Payton—that was her name—and I got along quite well. She was a little chatterbox. Started talking about her problems and asked if there was some place we could go and talk."

"Uh huh," Ed said, nodding knowingly.

"She told me to pull in here." The man pointed to the fenced auto repair shop.

"Okay. Then what happened?"

"Well, uh, Payton and I talked for a bit, and then she said she was really grateful to me, you know—listening to her troubles and giving her a ride and all. She wanted to thank me."

"Let me guess," Ed said, "You needed to unzip your pants for her to thank you."

"It wasn't like that."

"I'm sure it wasn't," Ed said, sarcasm dripping from his words.

"Mr. Milburn, what happened next?" Amber jotted notes on the card in her hand.

"Payton was giving me a…hug, when suddenly, someone tapped on my window. My back was kind of against the window. I jumped about a mile. She did, too. When I turned, there was a man standing there with a gun pointed at me. He told the girl to get out and take off." He pointed down the alley.

Amber nodded. "And she ran? Did he call the girl by name?"

Milburn looked confused, and shook his head. "Yes, she ran away, but no, he didn't call her by name. How would he have known her name?"

Ed sighed. "What happened after the girl split?"

"The man told me to give him my wallet, phone, watch, and even my wedding ring."

Amber spoke. "How long ago did this happen?"

"It's been about a half-hour ago. Forty-five minutes, maybe. I had to run back to the cafe to use their phone to call 911."

"What did the guy with the gun look like?"

"I'm not sure. He was wearing a mask."

"What kind of mask?"

"I don't know. It was black, maybe knit. I didn't get a good look because I was looking at the gun."

"How old do you think he was?" Amber asked, noting everything onto another FI. "What was he wearing?"

Milburn shrugged. "Like I said, all I could see was the gun."

"Okay. What did it look like?"

"It was black. And big."

She fought to keep her temper in check. "Was the barrel kind of boxy looking, or was it a revolver like the cowboys used?"

"Uh, I'm pretty sure it wasn't a cowboy gun."

"What about the girl? What did she look like?"

"I don't know. Young. Blonde hair, maybe five foot four. She had on a dark mini skirt and a pink top."

Ed tilted his head. "How young is young?"

The older man frowned. "Uh, I don't know." His cheeks flushed and his expression changed. "I know she was at least eighteen."

"You sure about that...*John*?"

The man blinked rapidly behind his bifocals. "Absolutely. Oh! She had a dollar sign tattoo on the back of her neck. Looked red, like it was new."

Amber nodded to encourage him. "And just how did you see the tattoo, John?"

Milburn bit his lip. "She uh, she dropped something, and I saw the tattoo when she leaned over to pick it up."

"Did you see the suspect's car?"

"No. No, I didn't. I heard it, though."

Amber tore the FI off her pad and handed it to Ed.

He stepped a few feet away and put out a crime broadcast describing the crime and suspect description to other units in the area.

"Now what happens?" Milburn asked.

"We're going to take a robbery report, and detectives will probably call you on Monday to follow up."

"How will I get home? The man took my keys, and I don't have my license."

You have a spare set of keys at home, right?" Ed smiled. "Give your wife a call."

Milburn gasped and shook his head. "I can't call Linda. She'd be mad as a hornet that I gave a strange girl a ride. How would I ever explain?"

"Well," Ed gestured at the surroundings, "you're parked at a car repair shop. You could tell her the car broke down and while you were trying to fix it, you got robbed."

"Hmm." Milburn chuckled softly and nodded. "That just might work."

"There's just one problem, John," Ed said. "I don't know how you're going to explain the lipstick smeared all over your fly."

26

DAZZLE

Dazzle had no trouble getting the john's wallet, phone, watch, and wedding ring. He ordered the man to put his face on the front passenger seat and count to fifty.

As soon as the old dude's head went down, Dazzle sprinted down the alley. He hoped that Candi figured out she should wait inside his SUV. *The girl has no street smarts—yet.* Seeing the outline of her head as he approached the vehicle, he relaxed a little.

He tossed his loot into her lap as he jumped in. "Open the glove box. I got some rubber gloves in there. Put them on before you touch anything."

Candi looked at the items in her lap. "What is all this?" Then realization must have hit her. She gasped. "Did you steal these from that old man?"

"What do you think?" He stomped the accelerator, kicking up gravel and broken glass as the Escalade tore out of the alley.

"Did you shoot him?"

"Geez, girl. Get a grip."

"Did you…kill him?"

He scoffed at her. "You watch too much TV. No, I didn't hurt him. I just liberated some of his property from him."

She stared at him. "You robbed him!"

"Yeah, I did. So what?"

Candi leaned away from him and waved her hands at the loot. "I don't want any part of this."

He jerked the wheel, skidded to the curb, yanked the vehicle into park, and leaned close, putting his face inches from hers. "You may not want to be a part of it, but you're in it up to your ass. If that trick calls the cops, you'll be on the hook just as much as I am for armed robbery. They won't believe you didn't know what was going to happen."

"I just want to go home." Tears filled her eyes.

"How the hell do you think we eat and have a place to sleep?

He leaned back and laughed in her face. "I wanna go home," he mimicked. "What? You think you're Dorothy from the Wizard of Oz?" He laughed some more. "Do you really think your parents will want you back now? You've used hard drugs, had sex with numerous men, been involved in armed robbery, and worst of all, you brought your little sister along for the ride. Your family don't want you anymore."

Tears rolled down the girl's face. "I don't care. I'm going home." She opened the passenger door.

The stolen items fell to the floorboard as he grabbed her wrist and wrapped his right arm around her neck, wrenching her upper body toward him and hissing in her ear, "I didn't drive all the way to Idaho to have you whining about going home. Get it in your head...I own you— you *and* your sister—and you'll do everything I say."

He shoved her back into the passenger seat.

Before she could even think about jumping out again, he drove off.

27

BROOKE

Brooke dozed off a little after midnight.

She'd set up a spot on the floor with the bedspread from the queen bed as her mattress and two large bath towels as blankets. She hadn't seen or felt any cockroaches, but they'd be preferable to climbing into bed with Dazzle.

Sleeping in the run-down motel was hard to do with all the noise in the neighboring rooms. People yelled through the doors, pounded on the doors, and slammed the doors. But noise wasn't the only thing that kept her awake. Brooke was worried about her sister.

At 4:00 a.m. Dazzle came back, and he didn't bother being quiet. He stomped around the room and into the bathroom. The sound of the shower soon started.

Heeding her sister's advice, Brooke pretended to be

asleep. *Where's Payton?* Maybe her sister was with the other girls in the other room.

"Keep away from Dazzle."

She was scared, but her sister's words kept running through her head. Brooke knew she was safer there, so with her knees shaking, she left her makeshift bed and fled to the room next door.

She knocked on the door with the pace of a machine gun.

"Who is it?"

Brooke recognized the voice of Sugar.

"It's me. Broo—um, Kitty." She felt a ray of hope when she heard locks being thrown.

The door opened and Sugar stuck her head out, looking up and down the open-air corridor. "What are you doing here? Does Daddy know you're here?"

Brooke pushed her way past the older girl. "I'm scared. Dazzle came back without Payton."

Sugar frowned. "Did he say where she was?"

"No. I pretended to be asleep."

"Does he know you're over here with us?"

Glancing at Diamond and Eden as they sat up in the bed they were sharing, Brooke lowered her eyes and shook her head.

"You need to get your ass right back to his room, or you're going to earn me a beating."

"I thought my sister might be here."

Diamond flopped back onto her pillow. "Well, she's not. Get out of here before we all get in trouble."

"I need to find Payton."

Something flashed in Sugar's eyes just before she

grabbed Brooke and hauled her onto the walkway outside. "Listen to me. Your sister is a lost cause. Save yourself." She relaxed her hold on Brook's arm. "You can stay in our room tonight. I'll square it with Dazzle. Then you've got to find your way home."

Tears filled her eyes. "I can't go without Payton."

"Kitty, if Dazzle didn't bring her home, your sister isn't coming back…ever."

28

———

ROY

Monday morning, Roy sat in the backseat of his pickup truck in the Foothill Division police station peeling a small banana for Gage, who sat next to him in his car seat. "Eat that up. Mommy will be here soon to pick you up and take you to school." He took a quick sip of coffee, bobbed and weaved while tying his necktie in the review mirror, then checked his phone again to see if Amber had texted.

There was nothing but a blank screen.

Damn it! I hope she didn't get stuck with a call at end of watch. He set his phone on the center console and handed Gage a second plastic baggie containing thinly cut apple slices. *I'm going to be late.*

His son chewed his fruit slowly as he focused on the employee cars entering the restricted parking area.

Black-and-white patrol cars began filtering in as the graveyard shift ended their day.

As each unit rolled past, Roy looked anxiously to see if it was Amber and her partner.

Enr to the sta now. ETA, 10. The text was from Amber.

Cops used abbreviations when messaging on their patrol car computers, and the habit carried over when texting on their phones.

Finally! He tapped *rog* on his phone, and relieved she was en route to the station, got Gage's hands and face wiped before his mother's arrival.

He'd just finished when she and her partner pulled into the lot. They parked in a stall and began unloading their equipment.

Her partner took the long guns, along with his war bag, into the station.

Amber carried her bag of gear over to Roy's truck. She looked tired, but then she'd been awake all-night. "Sorry I'm late. We had a john get ripped off by a girl and her pimp. We thought we might have tracked them down at one of the motels on San Fernando Road, but it was the wrong suspect and pimp." She grinned at Gage. "Just as well. I had more important people to see."

"No worries. If traffic isn't too bad, I should make it. I only have to go to Van Nuys."

Amber dropped to her knees in front of her son. "You ready for Mommy to take you to school?"

The little boy nodded.

"First, you get to come inside the police station while Mommy gets out of her uniform and turns in some paperwork."

The little boy grinned.

"Give Daddy a hug and a kiss."

Gage turned and raised his arms.

Roy lifted his son.

The child wrapped his arms around his neck and gave him a wet kiss.

"I love you, son. You have a good day and be a good boy for Mommy."

"Luf you, Daddy."

Roy looked at Amber and set Gage down. "Thanks a lot. I'm sure you're beat."

"No problem. I'll drop him off at school, catch a couple of hours of sleep, and pick him up again."

Roy nodded. "Gage, I'll call you tonight."

The boy nodded.

Without thinking, Roy leaned over and gave her a quick kiss goodbye.

She looked as startled as he felt.

"Sorry. Force of habit."

"I know. Some habits are hard to break." She smile, took Gage's hand, and led him toward the station's back door.

29

———————

AMBER

mber was tired and needed to sleep, but she was determined to make her time with her son count. She looked in her rearview mirror as she talked to Gage about his playmates in school and what he was learning. "What does a cow say?"

"Moooooo!"

She laughed. "That's great. Do you know what a horse says?"

He did a three-year-old's impression of a whinny.

"That's excellent."

Avoiding traffic on some of the major thoroughfares, she turned her car into a residential neighborhood, which was her usual route to Gage's preschool.

She came to a four-way-stop behind two other cars. They were most likely avoiding rush hour traffic, too.

Amber looked back at Gage. "What sound does a duck make?"

"Quack, quack." The boy giggled.

The first car went through the intersection, and as she pulled forward, the car moving perpendicular made a left turn. The driver apparently didn't see the man riding a bicycle across the juncture. He hit the bicyclist, causing him to roll across the hood of the car and fall to the ground.

The driver completed his turn and pulled to the curb.

"Oh!" Amber threw her car in park and sprinted toward the downed man. As she ran past the vehicle stopped in front of her car, she yelled, "Call 911." Amber knelt beside the man who had been struck. He looked to be in his early twenties. "Lie still. We have an ambulance coming."

The driver who'd hit the man came running. "He waved for me to make my turn!" He looked at the downed man. "Hey, man, I'm really sorry."

The bicyclist groaned and pushed into a sitting position. "I…I think I'm okay."

Amber shook her head. "Lie still until the paramedics get here."

"I've got some water in my car," said the driver and jogged back to his car.

Other drivers pulled to the curb and got out to see if they could help. Most vehicles slowly drove past the accident.

A woman with short gray hair and glasses knelt beside Amber. "I'm a retired nurse. Let me take a look at him."

Amber nodded and looked for the driver who'd hit the downed man. "I'll be right back," she said, pushing herself to her feet, and glancing toward her car before spotting the errant driver standing off to the side. The driver was also young, and he bit his lip and watched anxiously as others tended to the bicyclist, but she wanted his ID in case he decided to leave the accident scene.

As she approached, the driver locked eyes with hers. "Is he going to be all right?"

"I'm not sure. He's talking, and that's always a good sign." She closed the distance between them. "I'm an off-duty police officer. Do you have your driver's license?"

"Uh, sure." The kid pulled his wallet out of his back pocket and removed his license. "Here's my insurance, too."

While they interacted, Amber watched carefully for any signs he might be impaired by alcohol or drugs. She didn't see anything suspicious.

She automatically reached for her left breast pocket where she kept FI cards, but she realized she was in a T-shirt and jeans—not her uniform. "I'm sorry. I need to go to my car a get something to write on. I'll be right back."

"No problem," the young man said.

Amber heard an approaching siren in the distance. She'd bet money it was the RA—rescue ambulance—and hurried to her car. She'd jot down the guy's info and hand it over to the black-and-white unit when they arrived. *Quick and easy, because I know Gage must be wondering what's going on.* Smiling, she opened the driver's door, ready to reassure her son they would be on their way in no time, and looked in the back seat.

Gage's car seat was empty.

30

———————

ROY

As Roy traveled alongside hundreds of commuters on the San Diego Freeway, making their way through the San Fernando Valley, his thoughts ran through the various events that had led to Justin Lowe being charged with rape and multiple murders. The Feds were also going to try him under civil rights violations, since the sexual assaults had occurred while he was working as a police officer.

Ringing pulled Roy from his musings.

He glanced at his phone charging on the center console. The display read *Antonio.* He pushed a button on his steering wheel.

"Yo, Antonio. How ya doin'?"

"I'm good. Been busy."

"Yeah? With what?"

"I've got something for you. A new girl working the streets, says her pimp wants to start moving younger kids, which is saying something, man, 'cause at best, she's fourteen."

"That's great info, but I'm driving…on my way to court. Can I call you later today and get the details?"

"Yeah, sure thing."

"How's your work going?"

"Man, sellin' cars is tough. It was way easier slinging dope with the South Side Slayers."

"I get it. It doesn't help that the economy has taken a dump, but at least you're making an honest living."

Antonio chuckled. "Barely enough to live on. This straight life is tough."

"What about your sister? How's she doing? Staying out of trouble?"

"Yes, thanks to you. Araceli's working at that place on Sepulveda trying to get the working girls off the streets. I help, too, in my free time. That's how I met the young girl."

"I'm glad to hear it worked out with Araceli and Victims of the Street," Roy said. "Listen, I'm pulling into the parking structure at court. I'll probably lose you. I'll call you later."

"Okay…and Roy?"

"Yeah?"

"Thanks."

Roy smiled as he got out of his car.

He and the former gang member were unlikely friends after a terrifying and deadly incident involving his sister. Under Roy's guidance, Antonio had broken free from his gang, and also offered to be a confidential informant. The men's relationship was built on trust, respect, and killing a man.

There was a niggling worry that Antonio was hanging with working girls, but he'd get the details later. Right now, he needed to get to court.

PART IV

31

LACEY

Normally, Sergeant Lacey Galloway hated court. The wheels of justice turned slowly, if at all, forcing testifying officers to sit around for hours before they were called to the stand—or worse, dismissed when a plea agreement was reached. It was a colossal waste of time.

Today was different. Today was all about getting to know Detective Roy Buckner better, since she too, had to testify in the Justin Lowe case.

She walked through the courtyard in front of the courthouse. Dozens of people stood in the security line to get inside the building. There were a surprising number of children mixed among the stressed-looking adults.

"Galloway!"

She stopped and turned toward the sound of Roy's voice

and smiled in spite of the flash of disappointment that he hadn't called her by her first name. It was common in the work environment, but she hoped that with a dinner date in their future, he'd see her as a woman—not a cop.

The navy suit over a light blue shirt, brought together by a medium blue-hued silk tie, and topped off by his bright grin made him look like he'd jumped off the cover of a magazine.

"Wow. You clean up nice," she said.

He looked her up and down. "You're looking pretty good yourself." He motioned to a nearby outdoor vendor selling coffee. "Can I buy you a cup?"

"Absolutely."

"Have you given any thought to when you might like to have dinner together?"

She glanced out at the courtyard. "Sometime this week?" Her attention was drawn to a red-haired woman who looked to be in her forties walking toward the coffee vendor.

Most everyone nearby gawked at the woman striding toward the courthouse.

Her teal dress appeared to have come off the pages of a 1950s magazine, and caressed her every curve. The eye-catching neckline plunged to the top of her decolletage, where a fabric band gathered every inch of material covering her breasts. The ensemble was completed by a matching Juliet hat, purse, and ankle strap high-heeled pumps.

"I think we fell into a time machine. The only thing missing is the white gloves," Lacey said, feeling as though she'd faded into the landscape in her charcoal pantsuit, white cotton blouse, and black flat shoes.

The flamboyant woman stared at Roy until she was close enough to extend her hand. "Detective Buckner, so good to see you again." The bombshell tilted her head and looked at Lacey.

"Yes…it's, uh, it's good to see you, too," Roy stammered, as his face flushed. "Uh, Sergeant Galloway, this is Robyn McGee. She was married to Brent McGee, the brother of one of Justin Lowe's victims."

Robyn extended her hand toward her. "Delighted to meet you."

It took all of Lacey's resolve not to roll her eyes—the woman seemed to be playing a part. She gave the woman's hand a quick shake. "Nice to meet you."

Roy glanced at Lacey, then back to Robyn. "So, uh, are you here to testify on a case?"

Robyn chuckled. "I assume the same one that brought you here. Justin Lowe."

He cocked his head and frowned. "I don't remember you having any evidentiary information."

The woman shrugged. "I don't know. They told me to come…and I did." She smiled.

Lacey fought the urge to perform a gagging motion.

The vendor nodded at Roy, who looked at Robyn. "Would you like a cup of coffee?"

"That's very kind of you."

Roy held up his fingers. "Three."

Once they had their brew, the trio moved to a separate table where coffee accompaniments were available.

Roy's phone rang. He set down his cup and looked at the phone.

Lacey saw the display—*Amber.*

"Hi, what's up? I'm about to go insi— "His whole body tensed. "What? When?" He ran a hand through his hair. "Where are you?" He bobbed his head in frustration. "So, the police are there now?" He listened further. "Okay. Take a deep breath, and I'll be right there." He ended the call, grabbed Lacey's arm, and pulled her away from the table and Robyn's watchful gaze. "Gage has been kidnapped."

She gasped.

"I need you to contact the DA and tell him I won't be available until after we find my son."

"How did this happen?"

"I don't know. Something about a man hit by a car…I really…I've got to go. I'll call you when I know more." He turned and sprinted across the courtyard.

32

AMBER

At the scene, Amber spoke to the responding officers. "He's a male white, brown hair, green eyes, about three feet tall, and about thirty-two pounds. Three-years-old." She broke down, and the officers gave her a few seconds before pressing her for a clothing description.

After the officers put out a critical missing child broadcast, she paced outside the command post, also known as the CP. Invariably, her eyes searched the street for any sign of Roy's arrival as tears spilled and she tried to conquer the trembling of her body.

A police officer came out of the CP with a Styrofoam cup filled with coffee and offered it to her.

She shook her head. "No, thank you. I don't think I could keep it down."

The officer's radio squawked. "I've got a detective at the perimeter sayin' he's the boy's father."

The cop beside her keyed the mic attached to his shirt. "What's his name?"

"Buckner. Roy Buckner."

"That's him. That's him. Let him in," she urged, stepping away from the RV and looking down the street.

She sprinted toward him as soon as he came into view. His features were taut and his gaze darted over the area as if he thought that she and the dozens of cops at the scene somehow overlooked his son.

As they met, she threw herself against his chest.

His arms went around her momentarily, then he held her at arm's length, his eyes burning with anger. "How the hell did this happen?"

An officer stepped forward. "Let's go to the CP and we can tell you what we know."

Roy glanced at the cop. "I'm asking her."

"I was taking Gage to school." She pointed. "We stopped at the sign headed south. There were two cars ahead of us. One of the cars went through the intersection, and as the car ahead of me and I pulled forward, there was a bicyclist going east to west through the intersection. An eastbound car made a left turn and hit the cyclist."

"Then what?"

"I ran to help the guy on the bike."

"You left Gage alone in the car? What in the hell were you thinking?"

She wasn't expecting his criticism and began to cry again. "It was instinct. That's what we're trained to do. We help people."

"And you left our little boy alone and helpless in the car."

The officer took another step closer. "Hey, guys, we need to focus on finding your son."

Roy swung his attention to the man. "Are there any witnesses? Did anyone see who took my son?"

"We're working on that. Your wife has already given us the boy's description and what he was wearing. We're going door-to-door looking for witnesses and video."

Roy turned his attention back to her. "Did you notice anyone following you? Has anyone made any threats against you?"

"No, no, nothing like that." She broke down again and covered her face with her hands.

Roy looked at the cop. "What about the people who witnessed the accident? Did any of them see anything?"

"No. Everyone was focused on the guy on the ground…" He hesitated. "For what it's worth, everyone says your wife did an outstanding job."

"Oh, yeah? Maybe those people need to tell that to my son."

33

———————

ROBYN

After Roy's panicked departure, Sergeant Galloway reassured Robyn everything was all right, explaining that the detective was away for a family emergency. "I apologize, Miss McGee, but I need to go inside and talk to the DA. Nice meeting you."

"It was so nice to meet *you*, Sergeant Galloway." She thought she saw the sergeant roll her eyes as she turned and walked away. *Bitch.* No matter. With Roy off on a family emergency, however, it was unlikely the trial would proceed. "Things work out for a reason," she whispered as she unlocked her Mercedes SUV.

The dark tinted windows prevented her from checking the rear cargo section, so she opened the rear passenger door. "Excellent. No surprises." She started the engine and backed out of her parking space.

"These days you can't be too careful."

34

LACEY

Lacey entered the courtroom assigned to the Lowe case and saw the DA sitting at the prosecutor's table going over notes. A few spectators, and a couple of uniformed officers sat in the gallery. The jury box was empty.

She flashed her badge at the bailiff and passed through the swinging half-door entry that led to the counsel tables. She stopped beside the prosecutor.

The attorney was a handsome man in his fifties. His salt-and-pepper hair gave him the distinguished look expected of a lawyer. He immediately looked up. "Are you one of my witnesses on the Lowe case?"

"Yes," she said with a quick nod. "Sergeant Lacey Galloway, LAPD Internal Affairs."

The lawyer grabbed a list and ran his finger along the names. "Great. Thanks for letting me know you're here."

She bit her lip. "I'm afraid I have bad news."

A frown creased his brow. "What?"

"Detective Roy Buckner isn't going to be here. His so—"

"We've seated the jury; and we've started presenting the case. Unless he's in the hospital, he needs to be here." His tone meant business.

She took a step closer and kept her voice low. "Buckner's three-year-old son was kidnapped about an hour ago."

The prosecutor stared. "Shit," he finally said, under his breath. "Okay, stick around until I've told the judge. It's unlikely she'll force me to continue, but you never know." He thrust his witness list at her. "Is this the number where I can reach you?"

She glanced at the paper. "Yes, I won't be far."

"Good." He dropped his legal pad and strode toward the court clerk.

Knowing that cell phone signal strength was spotty in the court building, she made her way downstairs and outside. She wanted to call Roy, but hesitated. She opted for a text. *Any news?*

He answered right away. *Nothing.*

35

ROY

When Roy and Amber returned to the CP, a black female detective walked toward them.

"Detective Buckner, I'm the D-3 of Devonshire's Juvenile Table, Lavonne Duke. I'm in charge of your son's kidnapping."

"No disrespect, but I thought SIS handled kidnappings?"

"The Special Investigation Squad won't come in until we have a suspect for them to follow." She held out her hand. "How are you holding up?"

Roy shook her hand. "I'm focused on finding my boy."

"Believe me, we all are. Come inside. I need to ask you some questions." She led Roy past several detectives and officers seated at a narrow fold-down desk. Everyone was either talking on the phone or staring at a computer.

"When was the last time you saw your son?" Duke asked, as he followed her into a tiny room at the back of the RV.

"This morning, in the Foothill Division parking lot."

"Do you always exchange your son there?"

He shrugged. "Depends on our schedules. I have more latitude than Amber does. She's working patrol—currently morning watch."

"And Gage goes to preschool in Granada Hills, is that right?"

"Yes. The school isn't too far off the 5 or the 405 freeways, so we thought the location was a good compromise."

Duke leaned back in her chair. "I understand you and your wife have been separated for about a year and a half."

Roy nodded. "Yeah. We started divorce paperwork, but neither of us are fast-tracking the process."

"Are there any problems with custody issues?"

"No, not at all. Gage stays with me when Amber works weekends, and during the week, he stays with her."

Duke sighed. "Don't take this the wrong way, but is it possible your wife set up this kidnapping as a way to get you back or to hurt you in the divorce?"

"Absolutely not. That's ridiculous."

She looked away, tapping a pen against the table, then spoke again. "Most everyone on the department knows what happened to your wife several years ago. Is there any way that maybe she—"

"Amber would never hurt our son…and she isn't nuts."

"Okay, if you're that confident, I'll take your word for it. When I talked to her, I didn't see anything that concerned me either." She glanced at what he assumed were notes from the detective's conversation with Amber. "What about any cases *you're* handling? You're the department Sex Crimes Coordinator, right?"

"Yeah, but I can't think of anyone out to get me. It's not like I'm out there arresting suspects—at least, not that often." He rose. "I need to make some calls to my sex crime detectives and get them checking their files for possible suspects."

Duke shook her head and motioned for him to sit. "We'll get to that in a bit. Let's take a look at your personal life. Is there anyone who might want to hurt or scare you?"

Roy scoffed. "No, I lead a very quiet life."

The detective slowly nodded.

"Your wife told me about a former partner of yours— the woman you were having an affair with, Katie Nanako."

Roy shifted in his seat. "What about her? Katie would never do this."

"Have you seen her lately?"

"No. We talked on the phone maybe once or twice, but I haven't seen her since she left the department."

"Your wife told me Katie's little boy had died, and she took a liking to your son."

Roy exhaled and placed both hands flat on the tiny table between them. "Look. It's true. I had an affair with Katie. Amber never liked her. I understand that. But I'm telling you that Katie would not try to steal my son."

"Do you have contact information for Katie?"

Roy pulled out his phone out of his pocket, scrolled through, and gave her Katie's phone number and address. "I have no idea if that phone number is good or if she's even at that address anymore."

Duke nodded. "Your wife also said that when you came to pick up your son on Friday morning, there was a strange woman in your car."

"Geez." Roy sneered and shook his head. "That wasn't a stranger. It was Sergeant Galloway from Internal Affairs. We were both subpoenaed for the Justin Lowe case. We met to go over our notes and testimony." As he spoke, he recognized Amber's frosty attitude on Friday morning might have been instigated by his estranged wife seeing Lacey in his car.

Duke gave him a sidelong glance. "Is that all that's going on there?"

Roy sighed with frustration. "Yes."

One side of Duke's mouth lifted just a smidge. "Are you sure about that?"

"Yes, I'm sure, Detective…not that it's any of your business. Can we get back to finding my son now?"

36

———

DAZZLE

azzle rolled over in his bed, sorry that none of the girls were sleeping with him. He had an Olympic hard-on and didn't want to deal with it himself.

He looked at the floor. Kitty's bed was empty. He started to panic, but then remembered the late-night text from Sugar.

Kitty is missing her sister. She asked if she could stay with us girls.

His mind went to his evening with Candi...and how it ended. His morning boner deflated quickly at the memory, so he got up and headed to the bathroom.

After finishing his business, he headed back to bed, but was stopped by a soft knock on the door.

He threw on his pants and removed his pistol from beneath the pillow.

Holding the gun by his thigh, he opened the door a crack. *Kitty.* He pulled the door open and motioned her inside.

"Where's my sister?" the little girl asked, marching into the room.

He affected a cordial grin. "Good morning to you, too, Sunshine."

She looked at him with laser intensity. "Where's Payton?"

He leaned forward and frowned. "Don't you talk to me like that. Show me respect."

"You took my sister out somewhere last night, and she's not here this morning. Where is she?"

He straightened. "She's taking care of something else for me. Something that involves you, too."

One of Kitty's eyebrows lifted. "What are you talking about?"

He turned away from her and set the gun on the nightstand. "I realize you girls aren't quite ready for the life. I sent Candi out to look for a place for my new business. I'm starting a childcare facility, and you and your sister are going to be in charge of it."

He almost laughed at the girl's expression. "You've babysat before, right?"

She nodded. "Yes, I've helped out in the baby room at church, and babysat some neighbor kids. But Payt—Candi has more experience than me."

He nodded. "That's why I sent her to find the right location. She knows the perfect place to look for." He watched as she digested the information. "You're going to be the head babysitter. Do you think you can do it?"

"How many kids will there be—and how old?"

The girl's sharp. "I'm not sure yet, but you'll also have your sister available if you need help."

"Why won't she be in charge? She's older."

"Because she'll be working, like the other girls. I'll just have her help you at first."

"What if Pay—Candi doesn't want to do what the other girls do?"

"She makes a lot more money going out on dates. I told her, if she could earn the money, the both of you can go home to Boise."

Kitty's eyes widened and she smiled.

"Do me a favor, Kitty. Go tell Sugar I want to talk to her."

She nodded. "Okay. Will I see Candi today?"

He tilted his head, as though he was considering. "I don't think so. We'll see her in a day or two. Now go get Sugar for me." He grabbed his phone and began texting some of his buddies—putting the word out. He'd pay three thousand dollars for a kid under the age of eight.

There was a quick rap on the door, and Sugar poked her head inside.

"Enter."

"Hi, Daddy. Kitty said you wanted to see me."

"You need to get the other girls packed and ready to go. I want to be gone in an hour." He could see the questions in her eyes. "I found us a house. I'm tired of staying in these roach motels."

"What about Candi?"

He stiffened. "What about her?"

"Is she going with us?"

"No. You girls can divide up her stuff."

There were still questions in her eyes, but now her gaze also held a hint of fear.

"We rolled a trick. She threatened to go to the police. I had to teach her a lesson."

Sugar bit her lip and nodded like a bobble-head. "She just wasn't streetwise."

"Doesn't matter. You tell Diamond and Eden what happened. They need to know I won't stand for that crap." He pointed to the door. "Go get packing. You'll have to help Kitty—and as far as she knows, Candi is out scouting for a new place for us, understand?"

"Yes, Daddy."

"Be sure Diamond and Eden understand that, too."

AMBER

Four hours after discovering Gage was missing, an urgent tension replaced the chaos that had been at the crime scene. Uniformed police officers continued to report to the CP before filing back outside to widen the search for the boy. Roy was on his phone, pacing near the CP and urging each divisional sex crime detective to look for possible suspects in their files.

After his initial faultfinding, Amber gave Roy his space. He was right. How could she have been so stupid? As a police officer, she lectured people all the time to lock their car and not leave valuables in plain sight.

Tears filled her eyes again. She'd left the thing she loved most right there for anyone to take. *Gage.* She tried not to think of the terrible things that happened to kidnapped children. Images flooded her mind anyway, and her insides twisted with regret and shame.

Detective Duke stepped out of the CP. "Roy, Amber…" she waved them over.

Amber rose from her chair, and Roy took large strides to join them.

"Is there news?" She grabbed Roy's hand and held it tight.

"No, nothing yet." The detective cued a gentle smile. "We'd like you both to go home in case the kidnapper tries to contact you. There's nothing the two you of you can do here, and you'll also be more comfortable in your own space."

Roy's lips formed a thin line. "What about the FBI? Have they been alerted?"

"They're aware of the situation, but at this time, we aren't asking them to assist."

"Why not?" Amber snapped. "The more people looking for Gage, the better."

"It's still very early in our investigation. We're reaching out to the National Center for Missing and Exploited Children."

Amber caught Roy's gaze and knew he didn't think it was enough.

"We've brought recruits from the academy to search the berms along the freeways. We've got all Valley bureau senior lead officers and detectives concentrating on the homeless encampments, multiple air units are in the area searching, as well. The Mounted Unit is canvassing the nearby foothills. Metro Division is on their way, and if more officers are needed, we'll start pulling bodies from other bureaus." The gentle smile shone again. "Please, do yourselves a favor and go home. Try to rest." She motioned to the outer crime scene perimeter, where reporters and cameras crowded behind the yellow tape. "The media circus has begun. There's no reason for you to be a part of it. I've made arrangements to have you driven home." She looked at Amber. "Your car will be held as evidence."

"I'll get us home," Roy said. "Although it would be good to do so without the reporters tailing us."

Detective Duke nodded. "I can do that. We'll bring a van and get you inside and drive you home." She looked at Roy. "I'll get a plain-clothes officer to drive your truck home."

"Sounds good," he said, as he handed her his keys.

A uniformed officer poked his head out of the CP. "Lavonne, we've got video! The officer is sending it now."

Duke sighed and gestured for them to follow. "Come on. I know you won't leave unless I show you."

Everyone in the RV gathered around the largest monitor in the vehicle.

An officer worked the keyboard, and a black-and-white image from a doorbell camera filled the screen. The quality left a lot to be desired, but the view cover from the front porch to the street.

No one made a sound.

On the screen, a car drove southbound and then another. A few seconds later, pedestrians, moving north-bound on the sidewalk, came into view.

"That's Gage!" Amber shouted.

"I can't see the upper body, but the bottom looks like a man with him," someone said.

And just like that, they were gone.

Roy glanced at the officer manning the keyboard. "Run it again. Where did that video come from?"

The officer grabbed his radio. "17A45, this is the CP. Where'd you get that video?"

The unit responded with an address from the next block over.

"That's one block north of us," Amber said.

Detective Duke finished scribbling notes on her legal pad and looked at one of the uniformed sergeants. "I want officers canvasing for more video on that street and expand the radius four more blocks. I also want officers on the next four cross streets as well."

"I'm on it," the sergeant said.

Duke looked at her and Roy. "Now it's time to get you home."

38

———

LACEY

After the judge ordered a continuance in the Lowe trial, Lacey returned to her office at Internal Affairs. She worked in a satellite office located in the San Fernando Valley—in fact, not far from the site of Gage Buckner's kidnapping.

The office buzzed with gossip and theories, but Lacey wanted facts. She grabbed a department radio and tuned it to the tactical channel being used for the incident.

There wasn't a lot of traffic on the radio, mostly the CP verifying the location of the searching units.

It had been several hours since Roy's text. She grabbed her phone and sent him a message. *Have you heard anything?*

A few seconds later, her phone rang.

"It's me."

"How are you holding up? Can you talk?"

"I'm okay."

His breathing changed, and she could tell he was walking.

"Okay. I can talk now. It's Amber I'm worried about. I've never seen her such a mess. And, of course, there's a media circus here, so they're trying to figure out how to get us home without going through the gauntlet."

"It's a big story. I'm sure she's distraught. Is there anything I can do? Is there any new information?"

They found some video at a house a block away—Gage walking with a man."

"Is that the only video?"

"That's all we know. We probably wouldn't have known about it yet, except we were with the lead detective when she got the news." He sighed. "I swear if my son is harmed, I'll—"

"Don't say another word. You don't know who might be listening. Just let those who are assigned to the case do the investigating. You need to stay out of it."

He scoffed. "No need to worry about that. They're sending us home. They seem to think there could be a ransom request. I doubt that. You and I both know what happens when tiny kids are taken. They either wind up dead or as sex slaves."

"Stop. You don't know that, and it will drive you crazy if you think about it."

There was a long silence before he spoke again. "Did the judge continue the Lowe case?"

"Yes, until next week, but she seemed sympathetic, so I wouldn't worry until then."

"What happened with Robyn McGee?"

"What do you mean?"

"Did you explain to her what happened so she could go home?"

"I didn't give her details, just that you had a family emergency. I didn't see her after you left. I'm sure the DA's office called and told her to go home." *But I'd love to know why you're so concerned about Robyn McGee.*

39

ROSA

Rosa Juarez normally didn't answer her phone on her day off, especially in the late afternoon, but when she saw it was Robyn McGee, she took the call. The casting director sometimes called with a last-minute need for Rosa's services. She also paid handsomely for the privilege. "Hello, Miss Robyn."

"Hi, Rosa! Guess what?"

"I do not know."

"Logan is here! The lady from the adoption agency just left." There was a rustling noise on the phone. "Logan, don't touch that," Robyn shouted. "Sorry, he's exploring the house and was about to pull over the Waterford crystal vase."

"Children like to touch things," Rosa replied.

"Yes, I'm learning that. In fact, that's why I'm calling.

Do you think that you could come over tomorrow and help me get Logan acclimated to living here with me?"

"Um… what?"

"I know you have another client on Tuesdays, but could you possibly come over to my house and help me with Logan?"

Rosa thought quickly. She could get her sister to cover the Dorns' house tomorrow, and charge Robyn at a premium price.

"I can try, Miss Robyn, but will have to find someone to take my place with my other client."

"I'll pay you double. I really need your help. I had no idea little boys—Logan, don't put that in your mouth! Rosa, I've got to go. I'll assume you're coming unless I hear otherwise. Come at your usual time 9:00 am."

"I'll do my best, Miss Robyn."

40

ROY

Roy and Amber were driven in a white van normally used to transport the juveniles in the Cadet Program.

About two minutes after they arrived at Amber's house, a plain-clothes officer pulled Roy's pickup truck into the driveway.

He jumped from the cab of the truck, keys in hand. "Piece of cake." He grinned. "That reporter and camera guy from Channel 8 thought they were going to tail me. The cameraman was a good driver, but he didn't know the side streets and alleys as well as I did. Lost him before I ever hit the freeway."

"You must have hauled ass," Amber said. "You left after we did, and we just got here."

Roy opened the passenger door of the van and got out. He turned to the driver. "Thanks for the ride."

The officer behind the wheel nodded as the speed demon climbed into the passenger seat of the van.

"We're going back to the search. We're gonna find the SOB who did this."

"Thanks, brother." Roy slapped his hand twice on the door panel, then he and Amber went inside.

Even though it was only late afternoon, Amber pulled a beer out of the fridge and an already open wine bottle.

She took out two glasses from the cabinet and poured the beer into one, and half-filled her glass with wine before carrying both to the kitchen table and collapsing into a chair.

Roy scrambled to get his ringing phone out of his jacket pocket, he groaned when he saw who was calling, and tapped the screen. "Antonio." He'd forgotten to return his friend's call.

"Hey, man, I'm beginning to think our bromance is over. Were you ever going to call me back?"

Roy sighed. "I'm sorry." He then relayed to what had happened to Gage to Antonio.

"That's messed up, man. How can I help?"

"I'm not sure. Amber and I just got back to her house. We're going to eat and come up with a game plan. Why don't you come over and let's brainstorm some ideas?"

"You want me to pick somethin' up on my way?"

"Hang on." Roy looked at Amber. "What do you want to eat?"

"Pizza."

"I'll call in an order at that pizza joint right off the

freeway by our house. Can you pick it up? It will already be paid for."

"Yep. I'll be there in about an hour." Antonio hung up.

"Gage has been gone almost nine hours." Amber said. Her voice was flat.

"I know."

"He might not even be alive right now." She hung her head and wept softly. "*You* know what they do to kids."

"Stop it. Let's focus on what *we* can do."

She lifted her head and narrowed her eyes. "Sit and wait." She brought both of her feet onto the seat of her chair and wrapped her arms around her knees. "We wait until they come and tell us they've found his body."

Silently, Roy counted to ten. "Do you really think saying that is helping either of us?"

"It's the truth!"

They sat in silence…and drank.

PART V

41

BROOKE

After her talk with Dazzle, Brooke was mad—at herself.

She'd let him distract her with talk of being a babysitter rather than finding out what happened to Payton. Only after she'd left, had it occurred to her that Payton didn't have a car to go looking for a day-care place.

Wouldn't Dazzle do that himself? Where is my sister?

She knocked on the girls' door.

"Come in!" one of them shouted.

Sugar, Dazzle want you."

"Listen, Pee Wee, you're no better than the rest of us," Eden said. "You call him Daddy just like we do."

"I *am,* too. Dazzle is starting a day care, and Payton and I are going to run it."

The trio looked at each other and burst out laughing.

Sugar shook her head. "Oh, honey, you must have misunderstood." Her gaze shifted to the other two. "I'll go see what he wants." She chuckled as she left the room.

Brooke turned toward the other girls. "He's going to tell her what he just told me. Payton and I aren't ready for life— I don't know what he means by that, since we're both alive and living right now."

Diamond scoffed. "He didn't say you weren't ready for life. He said, you weren't ready to be *in* the life."

"I don't get it," Brooke said, shrugging. "Dazzle wants to start a day care, and because he doesn't think we're ready for life, he's putting us in charge of the kids."

The other girls frowned and locked angry stares.

"This is BS," Diamond muttered. "We work our asses off, on our knees half the night, while these two white bread girls babysit?"

"Damn right," Eden said. "Where's this tot lot going to be? You can't have a bunch of brats locked in a hotel room."

"I don't know. Dazzle said Payton was scouting out a location, but… I don't know how. She doesn't know how to drive and doesn't have a car."

Brooke left Diamond and Eden, cross-legged on the bed, whispering to each other, while she went into the bathroom. She needed time alone, because her instincts told her Dazzle lied to her.

She shut the door, reached into her underwear, and pulled out the business card and twenty-dollar bill her sister had slipped to her the night before.

After warning her to try to stay away from Dazzle, Payton had positioned herself between Sugar and Brooke. She'd pressed the card and the folded money into her hand

and whispered, "Don't say anything to *anyone!* Hide this in your underwear. This is how we're going to get home."

Brooke blinked back tears as she read the business card—*Victims of the Street…There is a way out.* An address listed in a city called North Hills was neatly printed at the bottom of the card next to a phone number. She didn't know where North Hills was or how she'd get there. "Payton, where are you?" she whispered.

When she heard Sugar returning, Brooke stuck the card and folded twenty between her belly and her panties.

"Hop to it, ladies!" Sugar yelled. "We're on the move again."

She flushed the toilet which drowned out any questions Diamond and Eden

asked, and washed her hands before exiting to find the other three girls gathering up their belongings. "What's going on?"

Sugar looked over her shoulder. "Daddy's found a better place. We're moving to a house. You need to go pack up your stuff."

"What about my sister? How will she know where to find us?"

Sugar rolled her eyes. "She's in touch with Daddy."
"How?"

The older girl pressed her lips together. "He bought her a cell phone. Now stop asking questions and go pack your stuff. Pack up Candi's things, too."

Brooke wanted to throw up. She didn't believe Dazzle bought Payton a cell phone. How would her sister ever find them? How could she find Payton?

When they pulled into a quiet residential neighborhood,

she was surprised. While the house wasn't nearly as big as her home in Boise, it was better than staying in a run-down motel.

Dazzle pulled the SUV into the driveway.

As they'd driven past the house, she noticed the grass hadn't been cut in a while and a "For Rent" sign tilted in the front yard.

He parked in front of the garage door. "Grab your shit and follow me." He headed for an open gate leading to the fenced-in backyard.

Brooke tried to manage her duffle as well as Payton's but couldn't carry them both.

Wordlessly, Sugar slipped the nylon strap of Payton's duffle over her shoulder.

Dazzle led them toward the back door, and Brooke immediately noticed that the pane of glass nearest the doorknob was broken completely out.

He reached through the hole and unlocked the door. "Welcome to our new home, girls."

42

———

ANTONIO

Antonio had met Amber and Roy about eighteen months ago. Amber had arrested him, but that arrest had thrust him into a position where he'd likely saved Roy's career, if not his life. After that deadly event, he and Roy, and to a lesser extent, Amber, had become fast friends.

He wasn't prepared for what he found at Amber's house. They looked like zombies. Amber's eyes were so red and watery she looked like she'd been smoking weed all day. Roy wasn't much better. He worked his jaw muscle so much he'd be lucky if his teeth didn't shatter. But it was the look in Roy's eyes that scared the former gangster.

He'd seen that murderous look in the detective's eyes once before…and someone had died.

He placed two cardboard boxes on the counter.

Amber unfolded from her stiff pose, and with glass in hand, she pulled the wine bottle from the counter and poured. "Beer's in the fridge," she mumbled.

"Plates?"

She opened the cabinet door on the way back to her chair.

Roy rose, pulled down some plates, slid two slices onto one, and set the pizza in front of her.

"I'm not hungry."

"You need to eat or you're going to get drunk. I need you sober, so we can figure out who would take our son and come up with a plan to get him back."

While they talked, Antonio grabbed pizza for Roy and himself and took the plates, along with a soda, to the table. "Did you say they had video of the kidnapper?"

"Looked like a man," Roy said, nodding. "Couldn't tell much and it didn't last more than five seconds. As far as we know, it's the only video they got."

"Did the department send you home?"

Amber nodded. "They told us we should be here in case there's a ransom request and that we'd be more comfortable." She scoffed. "They just didn't want us there when someone finds Gage's body."

"Amber, what's happened to your fighting spirit? I've never seen you just roll over and play dead." Roy took a swallow of his beer.

She frowned.

Antonio shifted in his seat. He didn't want to get in the middle of a fight between the two. "Hey, guys, let's do something productive."

Roy looked at him. "Like what?"

"Well, Araceli might know of someone selling little boys."

Roy winced. "Of course. Why didn't I think of that?" He looked at his watch. "Do you think she's still at the center?"

Antonio checked his watch, too and nodded. "She's usually there until about eight." He pulled out his phone and dialed.

Seconds later, he made a face and left a message asking her to return his call as soon as she could.

Disconnecting the call, his friends deflated before his eyes. "Listen, while we wait for her to call back, I can go back to San Fernando Road. I'll find that girl I was telling you about—Candi. She said something about her pimp dealing in young kids."

Roy made a face. "Street pimps don't deal in little kids. It's two different worlds. Besides, it's not likely she'll talk."

"I'm just telling you what she said." Antonio was annoyed with his friend's defeatist attitudes. "You guys could cruise Van Nuys Boulevard and Sepulveda and talk to some of the pimps. Pretend you're looking to buy a little boy. Those guys would sell their mother if they thought there was money in it." From the way they avoided his gaze, he could tell neither of them were excited by his plan. He leaned back in his chair and blew out a breath "Fine. My ideas suck. We'll sit here all night and do nothing."

Roy finished the last of his beer. "What are you doing picking up working girls in the first place?"

"When I have time, I help Araceli. The girls are afraid of their pimps seeing them talking to her, so I act like a customer, talk to them, and try to get information, or better yet, get them to leave with me."

Roy shook his head. "Do you really think some pimp is going to allow you to casually drive off with one of his girls?"

"Probably not, but I can try to build a connection so, in time, she'll let me help her leave."

Roy rose from his chair to get a glass of water. "You don't have time to build a rapport. They move the girls around quickly. The johns like fresh…faces."

Amber rose from her chair and looked at Roy. "Well, let's do something. Anything." She pushed her plate away. "It's better than just sitting here."

"I need to go to my office and look through our sex offender registrations and see what the sex crime detectives have found out," Roy said.

"Okay," Amber said. "You do that, and I'll go talk to the working girls and pimps."

"Absolutely not." Roy shook his head. "We'll go together. It's too early for the working girls to be out in full force. We'll go to my office first. I'll call the other bureau coordinators, and have them call their detectives, and *then* we'll hit the boulevards."

"All right. I knew you'd come around." Antonio smiled. "I'll try to track down Candi."

Amber stacked their plates and put them in the sink. "Let's hit it."

43

AMBER

Amber took the sexual offender registration card Roy handed her and ran the subject's information through the Master Inquiry database.

Roy had been going through files of required sexual registrants who were overdue for their registration. He'd give those cards to Amber to run for any recent contact with the police and the offender's last known address.

"That's the last of the overdues." Roy swiveled in his chair. "But if whoever took Gage is a sexual predator, he doesn't have to be an overdue. It could be anyone who's registered and with a penchant for little boys."

She held up a few of the cards. "Unfortunately, only these three have had contact with cops, and they all prefer prepubescent girls."

"Great. We've wasted a couple of hours and come up with nothing."

She pushed an errant strand of hair from her face. "We're not giving up. I'm sure your phone call to the bureau sexual assault detectives has them moving. Every division is probably doing what we're doing."

He nodded. "True, but it's Monday night, and it's late. The missing boy isn't their son. No one cares about finding Gage as much as we do."

"You're right, but we've got to try to stay positive. You work with those detectives all the time, and they like you. I'm willing to bet they're staying late trying to come up with a lead."

"Yeah, I know. You're right." He sighed and powered down his computer. "We've done everything we can here… in fact, we're probably duplicating efforts already underway. Let's give Antonio's suggestion a try." He rose and held out his hand. "Let's go see if we can find a whore or a pimp who knows where we can buy a little boy."

44

BROOKE

For the past couple of hours Dazzle directed the setup of the new house from his spot on the sofa. With laptop in hand, he ordered the girls where to put furniture, how to organize…everything. If there was a question or complaint, he shut it down by explaining this was going to make their jobs easier. "Kitty, go outside and write down the numbers off the front of the house."

She had to search for a pencil and took a scrap of paper from the overflowing trash can before darting outside to get the address.

When she came back inside, she held out the paper to him. "Will Candi be here soon?"

He snatched the address from her hand. "Are you stupid or what? I *told* you that your sister would be gone for a couple of days." He tossed the computer on the couch and hoisted himself to his feet. "Sugar! Get this kid away from me. I've got work to do." He strode to the refrigerator opened the door, and let out a string of expletives. "Diamond, get in here! Clean these roaches out of the fridge. I can't even get a soda without one of them bastards jumping on me."

While Brooke was aware of Dazzle's outbursts, she stood transfixed staring at the laptop screen. A picture of Payton, sitting with her back to the camera, sat on a chair spread eagle, wearing funny underwear that went up the crack of her backside. She was looking over her shoulder with her tongue paused against her smiling lips. The words plastered around the naughty photo: *HOT OFF THE FARM! Shy and innocent. Jasmine craves the excitement of the big city and ALL you have to offer. In-call only.* A phone number was listed at the bottom of the ad.

Brooke couldn't breathe. She felt flushed and weak-kneed at the same time and sank onto the couch unable to take her eyes off the disturbing image. Even though the screen said Jasmine, there was no doubt the girl pictured was her sister, Payton.

Sugar stomped over to her. "Get your butt off that couch. You can go in and clean the bathroom. Daddy wants us to work tonight." She glanced at the screen. "Aw, crap." The older girl slammed the laptop lid closed as she sat next to Brooke.

"My parents would be so ashamed of Payton," Brooke whispered. "*I'm* ashamed. I don't know what that picture means, but I'm afraid for her."

Sugar placed her hand on Brooke's knee and whispered. "Brooke, you need to forget about your sister. She's gone, but you need to get away from here. I'll try to help you if I can, but if Dazzle finds out, he'll kill m——."

Dazzle shuffled back into the room, a soda in his hand. "Sugar, I've already booked appointments for you and Eden. They'll be here in about a half hour." His gaze shifted to Brooke. "Go hang out in my room. There's a TV in there."

Shaken and numb, she nodded.

Dazzle turned away as his phone rang. "Yep. Hot, wet, and ready to ride." He listened for a few seconds. "When?" He listened again. "You got it. See you then." He looked at Sugar. "You girls are going to be working your asses off tonight. I should have done in-call a long time ago." He chuckled and rubbed his hands together. "Sugar, go get ready. Kitty, forget the TV. You go with Sugar and watch her and the other girls get pretty. You'll be having dates soon, too."

With her stomach churning, Brooke followed Sugar into a small room set up with a piece of board set on top of stacked cinder blocks. Above the makeshift vanity was a full-length mirror horizontally attached to the wall, so two or three girls could apply makeup at the same time.

Sugar started arranging her makeup. "Go get Diamond and Eden. Tell them we've got johns coming."

Brooke did what she was told, then followed the other two girls back.

Diamond scowled. "We've been fixing this place up all day. Daddy shouldn't expect us to flat-back tonight."

Applying false eyelashes to her dark brown eyes, Sugar shrugged. "Could be worse. We're not out on the street, and he's gettin' all kinds of calls for us."

Eden sighed. "Why the hell did he go all the way to

Idaho to pick up short stuff and her sister if he was just going to cut Candi loose? We'll have to work harder to make up her share."

"Maybe it's time Kitty learns why she's really here," Diamond said, her gaze finding Brooke's. "You don't really think Daddy brought you here to take care of kids, do you? He's going to make you have sex…with men. You'll learn to give them hand jobs, and suck their—"

"Diamond, shut up!" Sugar said.

Eden tossed her brush on top of the vanity. "She needs to know the truth."

Everything clicked into place. "You mean my sister was…was doing those things?"

Diamond scoffed. "Hell, yeah. She must not have been too good at it if Daddy dumped her already."

"Kitty, get your ass in here!" Dazzle called from somewhere else in the house.

A jolt of fear rolled through her. *What if he says I have to do nasty things with men?*

"Kitty, you hear me?" His irritation was clear, even back here.

"Yes. Coming!" She marched down the hall toward the front room.

Dazzle had pulled the sofa and two other chairs near the front door, forming a small seating area. At the top of the arrangement, sat a bar he'd dragged in from the den. He'd placed a lamp, a large glass jar labeled *TIPS* with a few dollars in it, and a tablet of paper with some kind of schedule on it on the surface.

"Go to the kitchen and find the plastic cups. I want you to fill about eight cups with ice, then store them in the freezer. If a customer has to wait for one of the girls, your job is to bring them a cup of water. We're going to run a classy place here."

"Okay," she said, relieved he wasn't making her wear weird underwear and do bad things.

She went into the kitchen and did what he'd said.

The doorbell rang.

She heard the front door open as she filled cups with ice and heard Dazzle talking to another man. Unsure if she should bring the glass of water, she stayed in the kitchen, but peeked around the corner.

The stranger was old, at least fifty, wearing a T-shirt and jeans. His fat belly hung over his belt.

Dazzle told him to sit while he got Eden.

The man frowned. "Eden? The girl I booked was Jasmine."

Dazzle displayed his *I'm a nice guy* smile. "Yeah, well, Jasmine took sick. Take a seat. I'm sure you'll like Eden."

The old guy didn't say anything, but flopped on the couch with his arms crossed, as Dazzle went down the hall.

Following his instructions, Brooke retrieved a cup from the freezer and added tap water. Her hand visibly shook as she carried the cup to the man. "Would you like some water?"

The guy's expression relaxed. "Well, thank you. I would. What's your name, sweetheart?"

"Um, Broo—Kitty."

"Like a *pussy*cat, right?" The man laughed.

She didn't know what he meant, or why he was laughing, but she was suddenly afraid.

Dazzle returned with Eden, who looked as pretty as

Brooke had ever seen her in a satiny robe, with her brown hair pulled into a ponytail high on her head.

"So, Phil…it'll be forty for the half-and-half," Dazzle said. He bobbed his head toward the tip jar on the bar. "Any tips for the girls go in that jar."

Phil smiled at Eden, then turned his gaze to Kitty. "No offense to Eden, but how much for the little kitty cat?"

45

ROY

As Roy and Amber cruised San Fernando Road, he tried to shrug off the idea hunting down whores and their pimps was a colossal waste of time.

"There's one. About fifty yards up. See her? Gold leggings and a black top."

"Yeah, I see her."

As he pulled about ten feet ahead of the young prostitute, Amber rolled down her window.

"You folks lost? Need directions?"

Amber smiled. "No, we're looking for something special and we're hoping you can help us."

The girl smiled, and then looked around, as if someone was pulling a prank, before turning her gaze to Roy's face. "Well darlin', what kind of help you lookin' for? I can fix most any broken man."

Amber pushed her hair out of her eyes and leaned out the window smiling. "Actually, it's for both of us."

The hooker grinned. "Hmph. I know men like to be in the middle of a girl-on-girl sandwich, but they don't usually bring the other girl."

Roy nodded. "We're looking for a boy. A little boy. The younger the better."

The whore grimaced and backed away from their truck. "That's sick. Get away from me." She turned around and walked back the way she'd come.

Roy pulled away from the curb. "Never thought I'd see a working girl with principles."

Amber sighed. "There's not enough action up here. Let's head over to Sepulveda. The girls work heavy over by that strip club at Roscoe."

"Fine, but if we don't get a lead within the next hour, let's go home and think of something else."

They hopped on the freeway, and fifteen minutes later, they were on one of the most well-known hooker tracks in LA. The girls walked or stood in groups of two or three on Sepulveda Boulevard. A few lone males stood watch, eyeing the street traffic and their girls.

"Try to find someone young, who isn't as street-wise as the gal up in Pacoima," Amber said.

Roy bobbed his head toward two girls walking together. "How about them? They're pretty short. Might be younger."

"You try talking to them first."

Roy pulled up alongside the two girls, a blonde and a brunette. His instincts were right. They looked to be about fourteen. He leaned over to talk to them from Amber's window. "Hey, ladies."

The girls paused and hesitated when they saw Amber.

"It's okay," Roy said. "This is my wife."

The brunette took a step closer. "What do you want?"

"I've got fifty dollars for some information."

"You don't want a date?"

"No, just some talk. You don't even have to get into my truck."

The blonde touched her partner's shoulder. "Come on. It's some kind of trick."

"No, wait," Amber said. "We heard that there's a guy who works little kids. Have you heard anything like that?"

"Come *on*, Paris. Daddy won't like this. They may be cops."

As if on cue, one of the men who'd been loitering outside a liquor store sauntered up. "Everything okay here?"

"He wants to give me fifty bucks for information about little kids."

The male's eyes narrowed. "You look and smell like cops. These girls aren't doin' nothin' wrong, just walking down the street, like any other American."

Amber nodded. "We're not looking to bust you or your girls. We heard there was a pimp moving young kids…little ones. That's *not* American. Have you heard anything like that?"

"It'll cost you a Benjamin."

"I'll give you fifty upfront, and if the info is worthwhile, I'll give you the other half," she said.

The pimp bobbed his head.

Amber handed him two twenties and a ten.

"There's a guy named Mickey D. I heard he put the word out he's looking for little kids. He'll pay three large per kid—more if they're real young."

Roy set his wallet in his lap. "You got any contact info for this Mickey dude, or know his true name?"

"Nah, turnin' out babies is bad mojo. I don't want nothin' to do with that. All I know is he usually works his girls on San Fernando, and his bottom is a bitch named Sugar. She used to work for one of my buddies."

Roy pulled another twenty and a five from his wallet. "Thanks, man."

As they pulled away, Amber rolled up her window. "Well, that's seventy-five bucks we could have set on fire for all we got."

"Yeah, I know. I just thought if I gave him something extra, he might come up with something else." Roy turned north. "Let's go back to your house. I'm fried. Maybe we can get a little shut-eye."

Amber shook her head. "Maybe you can sleep. There's no way I'm sleeping until my baby is home."

46

———

ROBYN

Early Tuesday morning Robyn had already downed two cups of coffee and then gulped two espresso chasers. She hadn't slept well.

Last night, she'd expected Logan to be so enraptured with his train bedroom and new toys that he'd play, get tired, she'd give him a bath, and then put him to bed. When that hadn't happened, she hadn't known what to do.

Instead, he played in his room for an hour or so, but was soon toddling around the house crying.

She'd tried giving him candy, and he'd slapped it out of her hand. When trying to cuddle with him, he'd wiggled and squirmed out of her arms. She'd finally resorted to the well-known trick of using an adult's liquid sleep aid to get the boy to sleep.

Such practices could be dangerous if the child was given

too much, but working with children in films, she'd long ago mastered the dosage based on a child's weight.

Her remedy worked fine until the boy was up and running before six.

Needing time to wake up, she sliced a banana, put in a bowl along with dry cereal, and put him in his highchair in front of a TV playing cartoons.

With the boy occupied, Robyn worked with haste, using the time to shower, dress, and put on her makeup.

When she emerged from her bedroom, the boy sat transfixed by the television and fingering rounded bits of cereal into his mouth.

"Logan, it's time to get you dressed. Rosa is going to come over today to help us. Won't that be fun?"

The child ignored her.

"Logan."

Nothing.

She raised her voice. "Logan, look at me."

The toddler shifted his gaze to hers. His lower lip trembled. "Mama," he cried.

"Yes, Logan! That's right!" Tears came to her eyes. "I'm your Mama." She swept over to the boy and smoothed his red hair from his eyes.

He started to wail.

She pulled him out of the highchair and hugged him close. "There, there. Don't cry."

The sound of a key unlocking the front door alerted Robyn that her housekeeper had finally arrived.

Robyn carried the boy to the entryway to greet Rosa.

The servant set her purse down and rushed to the boy. "*Que lastima, mijo?*"

Interpreting the housekeeper's concerns, Robyn frowned. "There's nothing wrong with him. In fact, you just missed him calling me Mama."

"Oh, Miss Robyn, he is so handsome. You didn't tell me he had red hair like yours."

"It's quite the coincidence, isn't it?" Robyn grinned. "How about we get him dressed and let him play in the backyard?"

"Yes. It's good for children to be outside in the fresh air and sunshine. I want to hear how your first night as Mama went."

47

———

ROY

After a night of fitful rest, Roy parked his truck outside the yellow crime scene tape surrounding the CP. The crime scene had been reduced once photos were taken, evidence collected, and Amber's car impounded and held for prints.

"I'm surprised they still have the CP in place," Amber said as she hopped out of the passenger side of his truck.

"I'm not. Our son is the lead news story in California. In fact, I'm sure it won't be long until the national news stations reach out to us."

Amber grimaced. "Swell. Just what we need."

As they ID'd themselves to the officer posted at the perimeter, Roy was struck by the anemic energy.

He yanked open the CP door and saw a lieutenant and several sergeants talking quietly around the table. "What the hell is going on? Why aren't you guys out there looking for our little boy?"

The lieutenant rose. "You must be Detective Buckner."

"Yeah, I am. What have you learned since last night?"

"Dan Gordon, Devonshire watch-3 watch commander." He looked at Amber. "You must be Gage's mother. I understand you're on the job, too."

"Yes. Do you have any new information?"

"We had our watch-3 officers out doing foot patrols at the homeless encampments, as well as reaching out to some of their unofficial informants in their areas."

Roy sighed heavily. "And?"

The lieutenant's gaze shifted to him. "Unfortunately, no one has seen a little boy matching your son's description."

Roy opened his mouth, but the lieutenant held up his hand.

"I spoke with Detective Duke, and she's arranged for an extension of the house-by-house search. The day watch will be handling that."

"Has any other video turned up with my boy and the man who took him?"

The lieutenant shook his head. "No. That's why we're doing the house-to-house search. Of course, you know people don't have to let us into their homes."

Roy and Amber nodded.

"What time will that start?" she asked, glancing at her watch.

"It already has. Detective Duke is out overseeing the deployment of officers." He nodded toward a full pot of coffee in the coffeemaker. "Why don't you grab a cup? She should be back any minute."

"Thanks." Roy filled two Styrofoam cups and handed one to Amber. "Let's wait outside."

Amber led the way, spotting several of her Foothill Division co-workers coming off the graveyard shift and checking out of the CP.

A couple of them came over to her and offered any support she might need.

"Thanks, guys." She pasted on the expected smile. "Go home and get some rest. You've earned it." Once they were alone, she turned to Roy. "So, basically, nothing has been done since last night." Her eyes filled with tears. "No one has seen Gage, and last night, we got absolutely nothing from talking to the working girls."

"It was a long shot at best," he said. Sighing, Roy scrubbed a hand over his tired face. "Let's hope Antonio did better than we did."

"Have you called him?"

"No, but now is as good a time as any." He pulled out his phone. After a few rings, he heard a mumbled answer.

"Mmm hm?"

"Antonio, it's Roy. Did you find the girl?"

"Give me a minute, bro. I need some water."

Through the phone, he heard shuffling and the sounds of swallowing.

"Okay, I'm back."

"Sorry to wake you. Did you see the girl?"

"No. I cruised both San Fernando Road and Sepulveda. I asked several of the working girls I've contacted in the past, and none of them knew Candi. And, of course, none of them knew anyone dealing in small children. Damn it, Roy, I'm worried about that girl. It was her first night in the game, and now she's disappeared. Something's happened to her. You need to investigate."

"I don't want to sound disinterested, but I'm more worried about finding my son."

"Oh man. I'm sorry. Of course, you are. What's happening in the search for Gage?"

Roy went through the lack of clues and the extended house-to-house search. "We want to talk to the lead detective. Then, I'll probably call a meeting with all the sex crime detectives…maybe Vice officers, too. Something better break soon. Every passing hour reduces the chances of finding my son alive."

48

AMBER

Whiile Roy was talking with Antonio, Amber's cell rang. She looked at the display. *Oh no!* With reluctance, she answered. "Hello."

"Do you have any idea how hurtful it is to turn on the news and see our grandson's picture on Good Morning America?"

"Mom, I'm sorry. We've been kind of busy."

"Too busy to let your parents know our only grandson has been kidnapped?" Ceci Granville's tone was incredulous. "How did you let this happen?"

"Mom, if you're going to berate me, I'm hanging up."

"Don't you dare."

Amber heard shuffling as the phone was passed to someone.

"Amber, this is your father."

She rolled her eyes. *As if I don't know your voice.* "Yes, Dad."

"Any news on the boy?"

"Nothing more than you saw on TV. As we speak, they're doing a house-to-house search of the neighborhood where he was taken."

"I think we should come to LA."

"Dad, that will only make it harder on Roy and I."

"Roy? This is probably all his fault."

"No, Dad. Gage was with me…it's all my fault." She couldn't help the warble in her voice or the tears rolling down her cheeks.

"What can we do?"

"Nothing, Dad. They won't even let us go out and look for Gage."

"I'll call the mayor's office. I'll see if I can light a fire under them."

"Dad, don't—" Her phone vibrated in her hand. "I've got another call. I have to go." Amber ended the call and looked at the screen. The display said, *Mission Detectives.* "Buckner."

"Hey, Amber. This is Kip Samuels from the Mission robbery table. I'm sorry about your son. Do you have a minute?"

Hmm, robbery detective from the neighboring division. Interesting. "Yeah. What's up?"

"I wouldn't bother, but your partner isn't answering his phone."

"It's fine. I'm glad for the distraction."

"Thanks. You and your partner took a 211 report from a guy named John Milburn the other night, right?"

"Yep, a trick-roll. Working girl named Payton and her pimp jacked the guy just west of San Fernando Road."

"Right. I've called the victim numerous times, but he's not getting back to me. Did he give you any more description on the girl?"

Amber sighed. "Not really. He said he was sure that she was eighteen, but I think that was to cover his ass. He originally said she was *young,* whatever that means. Why do you ask?"

"Because we've got an ADW victim at Hillside Hospital who refuses to give her name, but she matches the description on the crime report. She was beaten pretty bad." The detective sighed. "There's no way this girl is eighteen. More like thirteen or fourteen."

"Did you check for the dollar sign tattoo on the back of her neck?"

There was a rustling sound of paper. "Oh, jeez. I missed that on the report. I'll call and have the hospital verify the ink. Sounds like it might be the same girl."

"Can you text me back if she's got the tattoo?"

"Sure thing. I'll let the robbery table know what's up and get back to you. Good luck with your son."

As Amber ended her call, so did Roy, who told her about Antonio's failure at finding the young prostitute.

"Don't despair. I think I found Payton—the working girl who trick-rolled her john. She's in the ICU over at Hillside."

"Can we talk to her?"

"I thought you said street whores wouldn't know anything about child trafficking?"

"I still think that's true, but we can try. Clearly, they won't let us do much here."

Feeling the same frustration as Roy, she put her arm around his shoulders. "Look, I think they're doing their best. There just isn't much to go on yet."

"Let's go talk to the girl in the hospital. We can't make anything worse."

49

———

LACEY

Lacey badged her way into the kidnapping command post, and saw Roy and Amber were outside the RV, talking.

Amber spotted her right away. She must have said something to Roy, because he turned to look at her.

Lacey smiled and gave a half-wave. "Hi! How are you holding up?"

"Hi Lacey." Roy twisted his neck as though trying to crack it, and glanced at Amber. "We're hanging in there." His rigid body language screamed, *Go away.*

Maybe this was a mistake. She cleared her throat. "I, uh, just wanted to check in. Is there anything I can do? Any phone calls, errands…food runs I can help with?"

Amber brushed her hair from her eyes. "What's the

matter? Has IA run out of work trying to nail hardworking cops?"

"Amber," Roy said, giving Lacey a half-smile. "We're a bit tense."

"That's understandable."

"Roy! Amber!"

The trio turned to see Lavonne Duke marching toward them, a uniformed sergeant with her.

Duke came to a stop and eyed Lacey. "Who are you?"

"Lacey Galloway, IA."

Something flickered in the lead detective's eyes. "Lavonne Duke, I'm running this investigation. Is there something I need to know about this case that has Internal Affairs involved?"

"No." Lacey wanted to disappear. "I'm a friend of the Buckners. I came to offer support." She couldn't be sure, but she thought Amber rolled her eyes.

"If you don't mind, I'd like to talk to the Buckners. Privately."

"Of course." She looked at Roy. "Give me a call whenever you get a chance." She turned and walked away, overhearing Duke's booming voice.

"Who in the hell authorized you two hitting the streets last night questioning working girls and their pimps?"

50

ROSA

Rosa Juarez had legally migrated from El Salvador to the US when she was in her early twenties, with dreams of becoming a famous movie star and living in Beverly Hills. To prepare, she'd studied hard and learned to read and write the English language. She quickly learned that many people came to Los Angeles with stars in their eyes only to be victimized by callous predators who were quick to take their money as well as their soul.

After a year of costly disappointments, she resigned herself to housekeeping, and appreciated her time spent learning English. It paid off when she went looking for work.

The woman at the cleaning service she'd applied to immediately hired her, saying, "Americans expect their help to speak English. You'll get the better assignments." Her eyes roved over the young woman's body. "Watch out for the married men. They think they're paying for sex as well as a clean house. If the wife finds out, she'll fire you."

From the start, Rosa swore she wouldn't fall victim to her employers—male or female—although each gender had tried.

Now, twenty years later, Rosa had parlayed her earlier modest cleaning jobs into working for powerful people in Hollywood. She'd also learned about the dirty little secrets that kept Hollywood humming—alcohol, drugs, sex, just to name a few.

She'd only agreed to work for Robyn McGee because the casting director paid her well above what other clients paid, and the woman kept her home immaculate, which was why, just a few weeks ago, when Miss Robyn announced she was adopting a little boy, Rosa was shocked. In the five years she'd worked for the Hollywood heavyweight, the woman never once hinted at wanting a child.

Rosa had left the boy and Robyn in the backyard to go inside and make the boy a snack. He was a cute little one, but Rosa didn't know how her employer expected to cast films and care for the child at the same time. She was always working.

Seeing the kitchen trash can was full, she pulled the plastic bag from the container and carried it to the trash bin on the side of the house.

She lifted the lid, and was about to toss the bag inside, when she saw what looked like the shower curtain from Logan's bathroom.

She set down the bag of garbage, reached into the large plastic barrel, and pulled up the oat-colored shower curtain.

At first, she thought the panel was covered in blood, but she realized the fabric was stained.

A colorful cardboard box below the curtain caught her eye. It was a box of hair color—red. Odd, since Miss Robyn got her hair done at a fancy salon in downtown Beverly Hills.

Is it coincidence or a dirty little secret that Logan had red hair?

PART VI

51

DAZZLE

Dazzle realized he'd been a fool having his girls work the streets. They'd killed it on their first night of in-call service. Their last customer had left a 4:00 am.

He almost regretted the beating he'd put on Candi, but he couldn't risk cops finding her. She was too green to keep her mouth shut. *Stupid bitch had told the john they rolled her real name. It wouldn't take the cops long to find a missing person report for the sisters from Idaho.*

She might be history, but he had no problem using her photo to attract customers. And it worked. Almost all the calls he received were johns asking for Jasmine after seeing her picture on the internet.

A couple of guys had been pissed when Dazzle had

broken the news that Jasmine wasn't available, so he'd given them a price break.

Three johns wanted to book Kitty after they saw her, but he diverted their attention to his other girls. It made him realize he was losing money by not turning her out.

If an eleven-year-old is popular, imagine how much money a kid under eight will bring.

With all the girls still sleeping, he went to the kitchen and made some coffee. He sat at the card table that functioned as a place to eat, as well as his desk. Tapping on his phone, he reached out to a bunch of his street people, letting them know he was still interested in procuring young kids. He even upped his price to four thousand a head.

He'd also contacted his counterparts in Vegas and offered them the first shot at any little kids he got.

While Dazzle didn't want the headache of taking care of little kids, he had no problem holding them a day or two until he could offload them onto others who could use them however they wanted…for a profit, of course.

He planned to become the go-to guy for young kids. He worked out a sliding scale based on age—the younger the kid, the more he charged.

Looking around the poached rental house, he knew they couldn't stay long. It was a quiet neighborhood, and it wouldn't take long before the neighbors figured out what was going on and call the cops. If they got another few days here, the girls would make enough money for him to rent a house legitimately—a bigger house—to run both of his businesses.

He heard a noise in the hallway, and then the toilet flushed.

A short time later, Kitty shuffled into the kitchen.

He smiled at her. "Morning, Kitty."

She looked at him and nodded. No smile.

"Want some coffee?" He nodded toward the instant coffee on the counter.

She grimaced and shook her head.

"There's soda in the fridge."

"I'll just have water," she mumbled, pulling one of the red plastic cups out of the bag, filling it from water from the tap, then sitting at the table.

"I guess I should go out and get some donuts or something."

Kitty gave a half-shrug and took a sip of water.

"Actually, I think I'm going to send you and Sugar to SmartMart. You can take my car, whatever we need for watching young kids, and while you're there, you can also pick up some groceries."

"How many kids, and how old are they?"

He took a sip of coffee from the mug he'd found in one of the cabinets. "Don't know yet."

"Where are they coming from?"

"You don't need to worry about that. All you have to do is watch them."

She took another sip of water, then stared off into space. "When will I get to see Payton?"

"I'm not sure...and call her by her new name."

"I'm going to get dressed," she said, standing.

Dazzle looked at his watch. "I'm going to give the girls another fifteen minutes, and then I'll get them up. Be ready to go out with Sugar."

She nodded and scuffed toward the bedrooms.

That one might be the big moneymaker, but she's also going to be the biggest pain in the ass. Maybe you should break her in and show her who's in charge.

The more he thought about the idea, the better he liked it.

52

ROY

After Lavonne Duke ripped Amber and Roy new orifices, she ordered them to go home and to stay out of her investigation.

The chewing out was barely a blip on his radar. The day was young and already out of control, and he was wrapped tighter than a nylon leg restraint secured to an arrestee's ankles. Concern for his son, and lack of sleep were taking a toll. Lacey's appearance offering support couldn't have come at a worse time. It didn't help that Amber was acting like a jealous wife. *Hello…we're getting a divorce, remember?* Amber's voice pulled him from his worries.

"What can Duke do to us if she finds out we're still working on Gage's disappearance?"

"Do you really give a rat's ass? He's been missing for

over twenty-four hours. We both know that isn't good. I'm not putting our son's life in someone else's hands."

Her phone vibrated with a text message. "It's from Samuels at Foothill. The girl has the tattoo. She's likely the gal who robbed her trick. They'll do a photo lineup if they can ever get hold of the robbery victim."

Roy increased the pressure on the accelerator. Hopefully, this girl would give up some helpful information about Gage to garner favor regarding her part in the robbery. Of course, he and Amber couldn't make her any binding promises—but the hospitalized girl didn't have to know that. All he cared about was getting Gage home safe.

"I think you should let me do the questioning," she said.

"Let's play it by ear. I've had a lot more experience conducting interviews, but she may relate better to you."

A few minutes later, they badged themselves into the ICU and stood next to the young girl's bed. Eggplant-colored bruises covered the girl's face, arms, and even her throat.

"Man, somebody really worked her over," Amber whispered. "Even if we got pictures of her, I don't think the robbery victim would be able to ID her."

Roy moved closer to the head of the bed. "Hey, can you hear me?"

There was no reaction from the girl.

He tried again. "Can you hear me? Open your eyes."

"Let me try." Amber moved to the other side of the bed and took the teen's hand in hers.

"You try to get through to her. I'll talk to the staff and get whatever info they have on her." Roy headed for the nurse's station.

Staff moved in and out of the area with haste.

Finally, a woman in scrubs took notice of him. "Can I help you?"

He showed her his ID. "Yes, I'm Detective Buckner, LAPD. I'd like any information you have on the assault victim, in bed eight."

The nurse shook her head. "We don't have a lot. She came in unconscious and unstable. We tried stabilizing her, and her blood pressure crashed. It was touch and go for a couple of hours, but she seems to be out of the woods now. She won't give us a name, so she's Jane Doe. Because of her tattoo, the way she was dressed, and a purse full of condoms, we're keeping her in the ICU as a precaution. We don't want her pimp coming in and taking her out to flat-back at some seedy motel."

"Was she transported by RA?"

The woman sighed and pulled up a file on the computer. "I'm sorry, I can't stay and answer all your questions, but I'll print out what we've got on her." She tapped a few keys and grabbed several sheets of paper from the printer on the counter behind her. "You're not supposed to have the medical information, so I'd appreciate it if you'd shred these before you leave." She handed him the pages,

and bobbed her head at a shredder against the wall.

"You got it," he said.

The woman hurried off.

He read through the paperwork, then returned to the girl's bedside.

Her eyes were open

Amber leaned close to her face. "Who did this to you? Was it a date?"

The girl moved her head side-to-side slightly and closed her eyes.

Amber looked at him.

He motioned for her to follow him.

"I have to leave for a few minutes, but I'll be right back." Amber gave the girl's hand a squeeze and came over to him.

He opened the door and stepped out into the hallway and turned to his estranged wife. "Did she give you any info about Gage?"

"No. She won't give me her name. She's scared. I don't think she'll throw her pimp under the bus, but I'm betting he's the one who did this. What did *you* find out?"

"She was brought in, unconscious, by ambulance from Sepulveda and Plummer. Her blood pressure crashed." He looked up from the paperwork. "They thought she might have serious internal injuries, but found nothing, and she's bouncing back. They're keeping her in the ICU, so her pimp doesn't come get her and put her back out on the streets."

"What about the cops who were called to the scene? Do we have their report?"

"No, but we aren't far from Mission Station. We can get a copy."

"Have them email you one."

Roy shook his head. "You know how it is. They'll take a half hour to determine I'm who I say I am. It's faster to go get it. What did you say his name was…the Mission D-3?"

"Kip Samuels."

"I'll talk to him. Maybe he'll have more info. What are you going to do?"

"I'll try to get the girl to tell me who she is and what

happened to her. She dozes off a lot. I thought she said something about a little girl, but she nodded off."

"Okay. I'll be back in about forty minutes."

53

BROOKE

Brooke was braiding her hair in the bathroom when, true to his word, Dazzle came into the bedrooms and yelled at the other girls to get out of bed.

She heard all three of them groan about needing more rest.

"Don't give me that crap," he said. "I could have had you walking the street out in the cold. All you had to do here was take care of the johns."

"Yeah? Well, it would have been nice if you'd come in a little sooner when my john was using me as a punching bag," Diamond complained.

Brooke heard fast stomping and then the sound of flesh meeting flesh.

"I'm sorry. I'm sorry, Daddy! Stop it."

"You don't like to get beat? Maybe you mouthed off to your john too. Maybe that's why he placed hands on you."

At the sound of more blows landing and Diamond crying, Brooke set the brush down and placed her hands over her ears. She got under the homemade vanity and made herself as small as she could.

Eden burst in and started the shower, while Sugar carried clothes into the bathroom, slamming the door behind her.

"Damn 'ho don't know when to keep her mouth shut," Eden muttered and looked down at Brooke. "What the hell you doin'? You think Daddy can't find you down there?"

She buried her face into her hunched knees. "I want to go home."

"Yeah, and people in hell want ice water."

She ignored the older girl—of all of them, Eden was her least favorite—and took her hands away from her ears. There was an eerie quiet in the bedroom.

Then…she heard grunting and then a moan. *Was Dazzle killing Diamond?*

"Good thing Diamond's taking care of Daddy this morning, or he'd probably be coming for you," Eden said leering at her.

"What do you mean?"

"What do you think is going on in there? Diamond's suc—"

"Eden, shut your mouth. She doesn't need that information." Sugar glared at the other girl.

"I'm getting sick and tired of you protecting this girl. You got her thinking you're some kind of hero and better than me. You're always telling me what to do, Sugar. You don't own me."

"No. I don't. Daddy does. And if we start fighting with each other he's going to beat us all," she said, brushing her hair. "We made a bundle last night and you can bet he's going to have us working every night for a while. We can't afford to be anymore sore than we already are." Sugar looked at Brooke. "Come up out of there."

A primal groan burst forth from the room across the hall.

Eden and Sugar exchanged a glance as the little girl crawled out from her hiding place and Diamond ducked into the bathroom with bright red marks lining her face, neck, and arms.

A few seconds later, Dazzle pushed the door wide open as he adjusted the waistband of his pants. Seeing all four girls in the makeup room, he frowned. "Sugar, come with me. I have a job for you and Kitty. You two are going shopping."

54

ANTONIO

After his phone call with Roy, Antonio got showered and dressed. Having a few hours before he had to be at the used car lot, he drove to Victims of the Streets.

The facility, was a center where people working the streets, male, female, adults, and kids, could come for help to leave the vicious circle of selling their bodies...and their souls.

Just as he'd helped Antonio find a job, Roy had gone to bat with the founder of Victims of the Streets for Araceli. A former working girl and stripper, Araceli was scared straight when Antonio and Roy saved her from being murdered by a former abuser.

He walked through the door where one of the teen residents sat at the front desk, eyeing his gang tattoos.

"Hi there! I'm Araceli's brother. Is she here?"

"Your name, sir?"

He grinned. "Antonio. Although if you tell her it's her pain-in-the-ass brother, she'll know for sure it's me."

The girl giggled and dialed the phone. "Your brother, Antonio, is here to see you," she murmured. "Okay." She hung up and smiled. "She said you should go to her office. Do you know the way?"

He smiled. "I do. Thank you." When he reached the door marked *Counselors* he tapped and poked his head inside the room.

Araceli looked up from where she sat, typing behind a computer. "Come on in." She pushed back from her desk and motioned for him to take a seat in a chair beside of her desk.

"I feel like I'm back at school about to get chewed out by the principal."

"What are you doing here?"

"I suppose you've seen the news about the Buckners' little boy."

His sister's face sobered. "Yes. I was going to call you, but it's been busy this morning. I feel awful for them. Do you have any news?"

"Nah." He shook his head. "They did a house-to-house search in the neighborhood, but there's no sign of him."

"What brings you here?"

"You didn't return my call from last night. I was wondering if any of the girls ever talk about anyone dealing in little kids—young, like Gage Buckner's age. You hear any chatter like that?"

Araceli sighed. "For the past few months, the gangs have

focused more on human trafficking than drug smuggling. It's easier to get kids over the border than dope."

He nodded. "I'm looking for someone dealing specifically with younger kids."

"Maybe…a little girl who came in just a little while ago."

"Why do you think she'd know baby traders?"

"Because she's not much older than a baby herself. Maybe ten or eleven years old. She wouldn't give me a lot of information."

"Is she here? Can I talk to her?"

Araceli shook her head. "Nope. She came in but was clearly scared to death. She's been staying with a pimp and his girls, but for some reason, he hasn't turned her out yet. She wanted help finding her sister but wouldn't tell me anything to go on. I pushed her for info. She freaked and took off in a black SUV driven by a black girl."

"We're your cameras able to pick up the license plate on the ride?"

His sister scoffed. "Those cameras haven't worked in at least a month. There's no money to get them fixed."

He gave her a reassuring smile. "Well, she came in once, so I bet she'll come back. Did she give you her name?"

His sister shook her head. "Just her first name, Brooke." Araceli sighed. "And the sister's name is Payton."

55

___

ROBYN

Robyn caught the Hispanic woman's gaze focused on Logan's face more than once, and thought she might have made a mistake having Rosa come to help her take care of Logan. It didn't help that the little boy kept pulling off the eyeglasses she'd bought for him.

Robyn sat at the kitchen table with the boy, encouraging the toddler to eat the peanut butter and jelly sandwich Rosa had cut out with a star cookie cutter. She put grapes and a yogurt tube alongside the star sandwich pieces.

Logan ate the fruit and bit off pointy pieces of sandwich before pulling his tortoise-rimmed glasses from his face and tossing them to the ground.

"I've told you, Logan, you have to leave your glasses on," she said, resting the plastic frames on his nose and ears. "They help you see."

The boy shook his head and flung the eyewear to the floor.

"Shame on you! You're a bad boy."

Suddenly, Rosa appeared. "Miss Robyn?"

"Yes. What is it?" Her tone sounded testy even to her.

"Since I'm here today, I thought I would touch up Logan's bathroom. I see the shower curtain is missing."

"Um…yes. I was watching Logan in his bath. I had a cup of coffee and spilled it all over. Fortunately, the curtain got the most of it and the plastic liner spared Logan. I had to throw the shower curtain out. There's definitely a learning curve with little ones in the house." She smiled at the maid. "I'll get a new one in the next few days."

Rosa smiled and nodded. "Very good, Miss."

As the housekeeper walked away, Robyn's heart lurched. The usually subservient smile Rosa kept on her face appeared to be a smirk. *Don't freak out. You're just tired. You had no sleep last night.* She looked at the little boy playing with what was left of his sandwich. "Logan, let's wash your hands, then we'll go into your bedroom and play with some toys."

The boy, not moving, watched her.

She smiled and held out her hand. "Come on. I'll let you stand on a step stool at the sink."

The boy sat at the table and continued staring.

She retrieved the plastic stool from the pantry and placed it in front of the sink. "Come on. It will be fun," she said, turning on the water and motioning him closer.

Slowly, the boy slid from his chair and pulled himself up the two steps to wet his hands in the sink.

AMBER

After Roy left for Mission Division, Amber sat in Jane Doe's room, near the bed, and watched her, trying to imagine what she'd look like without the vivid bruising and swelling covering most of her face and body.

Even wearing a miniskirt and boots, there was no way *any* trick would think she was eighteen. She didn't look more than fourteen. Of course, during Amber's time working the streets, most johns she'd arrested said, when they hired a working girl, they didn't even look at her face.

The nurse came in to check the girl's vitals and see if she needed anything.

She stirred at the activity, opening her eyes to a slit.

"Hey, sweetheart. You need anything?

The girl closed her eyes.

"I'm going to put this call button in your hand. If you want something, you press the button and I'll come." The nurse turned to Amber. "Good luck."

Amber stood next to the bed and took the girl's left hand. "I'm Officer Buckner of the Los Angeles Police Department."

The girl's eyes blinked open.

"I'm here to find out who did this to you."

"I don't know," she murmured, pulling her hand away.

"I think you do." Amber sighed. "I think you rolled a trick the other night off Kelowna and San Fernando."

The girl winced as she shook her head. "I don't know what you're talking about."

"You and your pimp picked the wrong guy to roll. We've got you on video, and your date is ready, willing, and able to ID you in court." She pulled a chair next to the bed. "But maybe I can work with you a little."

"I don't even know what you mean about *rolling someone.*"

"I think your pimp beat you, and I think your name is Payton."

"I'm not a prostitute…and my name isn't Payton," she mumbled.

"Then, what *is* your name?

The girl stared at her.

"Look, I'm offering you a chance to possibly work a deal on an armed robbery. If you're convicted—and you would be—you're looking at some serious prison time."

The girl's eyes widened. "Prison? I haven't done anything wrong! I didn't know what was going to happen."

"Listen, you're not the first young working girl I've dealt with, and sadly, you won't be the last." Amber rubbed her fingers over her lips as she eyed the girl. "From the looks of you, you haven't been in the life too long. I can put in a good word with the district attorney so, maybe, we can get your robbery charge dropped down to some kind of misdemeanor. Then, you can do some community service rather than spending any time in a group home."

Large tears slid down the girl's bruised cheeks. "I don't know what a group home is, but I don't want to go there. I just need to get out of this hospital and back to my…my…"

"Your pimp? The one who put you in here? Are you insane? You can't work the streets in the shape you're in. You were touch and go when you were brought in."

"I have to get back there. Then I'll leave him."

Amber shook her head and sighed. "I'm looking for information on anyone trafficking young children."

"Why would I know anything about that?"

"Because you deal with whale shit…the dregs from the bottom of the ocean. That means you rub elbows with sick bastards who think it's okay to rape little kids—and I'm not talking about children your age. I'm talking about babies and toddlers." Amber knew she'd touched a nerve when more tears filled the girl's eyes. She stared at the girl praying she'd decide to talk.

"Leave me alone. I don't know anything about little kids." The girl's tone sounded so defeated.

"You're only hurting yourself. You'll be arrested for armed robbery."

"Get out. I can't talk to you."

"Fine." Amber sprung from her chair and put her face mere inches from the girl's startled expression. "You don't have to talk to me. Keep protecting your pimp. But let me tell you something—any chance of me helping you, or asking the DA to offer you a deal, walks out the door with me."

"I can't help you," the girl said softly, then turned onto her side.

Amber grabbed the girl's shoulder and gently pulled her around to face her. "Listen to me. I understand that you're scared, but somebody has kidnapped my little boy. I'm hoping you might know something."

"Someone took your little boy?"

Amber, regretting her outburst, nodded. "Yes. Truth is… I don't give a damn about you, or your pimp, but I do care about my little boy. You can either help me, or I can throw you under the bus for robbery." She released the girl's shoulder. "I'm willing to bet you've never been in jail, much less prison. But let me tell you, felony juvenile detention isn't like high school. It's a whole other world."

"I'm sorry."

"Then help me…*please.*"

The girl shut her eyes. "I'd help you if I could, but I can't."

57

ROY

Roy hoped Amber's interview with the Jane Doe was going well, because he was returning to the hospital with nothing useful.

The reports from Mission Division weren't particularly helpful. Officers had responded to a "woman down" radio call. The report showed where they'd found Jane Doe, the RA's number, and the names of the paramedics taking her to Hillside Hospital. The girl was in no shape to be questioned, so there was no real investigation, merely the details of the pickup and delivery of a severely beaten teen girl.

His talk with Kip Samuel hadn't brought forth any additional useful information, either.

As he strode to Jane Doe's hospital room, Amber was just coming out.

"Hey," he said. "Any luck with her?"

Amber shook her head and bit her lip. "The girl was almost beat to death by her pimp, and she won't give up anything about him, and won't even give me her name."

Roy felt the waves of frustration radiating off her.

There was a time he would have taken her in his arms and comforted her, but thanks to his affair, those days were gone. No matter what he'd done, though, the fact remained that his feelings of concern—no, his feelings of *love* for his former wife were still present.

He ran a hand through his hair. "Maybe we're just spinning our wheels here. We have no real reason to think this girl knows anything about trafficking of small children. All she knows is how to work the streets and turn her earnings over to her pimp."

Amber's head jerked up. "Maybe *that's* where we need to concentrate our time. Instead of trying to get this kid to talk, let's find her pimp and arrest his ass for the robbery. He'd be more likely than her to know about trafficking children."

"That's a great idea, but if you're right about the pimp being the one who put the beat-down on this girl, he's probably lying low."

He was surprised when she gave him a light punch in the arm.

"Come on. We're big city cops. Heck, you're a seasoned veteran detective. I think we've got what it takes to find a pimp robbery suspect, especially since Gage's life depends on it."

Her phone rang, and she held it out so he could read the display: *Lavonne Duke.*

58

———

PAYTON

Payton tried to sleep, but she kept thinking about Brooke. Her first order of business was getting well enough to leave the hospital. Then, she'd get her sister and go back home to Boise.

Lying in the hospital room alone, she recounted the past few days. Dazzle didn't love her. He charmed her away from her home, family, and church with all the right words, only to hand her over to his friends, to be beaten, degraded, and filled with shame.

Payton felt terrible for the lady cop and her missing little boy. She seemed nice—even though Dazzle said the police were the enemy, arresting girls just trying to make an honest living.

Yeah, but Dazzle is a liar and a robber, which isn't an honest living.

She hadn't known that he was going to rob her john, the cop had made it clear she could wind up in jail for her part in it.

But…I can't go to jail.

She had to find Brooke before Dazzle made her little sister do the same horrible things he'd forced onto her.

A nurse breezed into the room. "Glad to see you're awake. You'll be happy to know that the doctor said that we can remove your IV, and tomorrow, they'll probably move you out of the ICU."

"Has…has anyone come to see about me?" The look on the nurse's face—the soft eyes and the sad smile—told Payton everything she needed to know.

"If you were expecting your, uh, boyfriend, he probably won't come anywhere near the hospital. The police want to talk to him."

The police! What if Dazzle takes Brooke and goes on the run?

She *had* to get out of this hospital and find her sister and go home. She'd be on the run, too, but the police wouldn't know to go to Boise.

Would they?

Her heart dropped at the thought of seeing her parents. Dazzle said, if she went back, they would hate her—and he was right. She was a prostitute with a tattoo on her neck. Worse yet, she dragged her little sister into a life of degradation, lies, and perversion.

They'll hate me forever.

Even if they didn't, how could they possibly take her back? The gossip and shame—for the whole family —would come from everyone throughout the church and throughout the town.

Her stomach lurched again at the thought of Dazzle being alone with her sister. She had to go get Brooke and go somewhere…anywhere. Maybe home, maybe not.

But how?

59

———

ROSA

Thanks to her clients, Rosa had seen almost every kind of cosmetic alteration possible on a human body. But even by Hollywood standards, coloring a toddler's hair and forcing him to wear unneeded glasses seemed extreme.

Miss Robyn should be ashamed! Smiling at the knowledge of her new dirty little secret, she went about her business tidying the house.

Robyn's voice in the hallway alerted the housekeeper that her employer and probably the boy were coming toward Logan's bedroom.

Rosa finished tossing some toys into a toy box, then she smiled as the pair entered the bedroom.

"Oh, good, you're here," Robyn said. "I want him to take a N-A-P. How do you think I should go about it?"

Que' idiota. "Tell him it's time for a N-A-P. Take off his shoes, and have him lie down in the bed."

"But what if he gets up?"

Rosa grinned. "You put him back."

Her employer frowned. "I don't have all day to play Johnny jump-up with him."

Rosa shrugged, realizing her boss had no idea what caring for a child entailed. Robyn would learn soon enough she'd made a huge mistake by adopting the boy.

Irritation flashed in Robyn's eyes, and she turned to him. "Logan, it's time for you to take a nap. Mommy has to get some work done."

Logan's lower lip quivered, and his eyes filled with tears.

Robyn carried the boy to the bed, plopped him on the mattress, and pulled his shoes off. "Lay down and rest. You'll feel better if you take a break."

Standing behind her boss, Rosa fought to contain her grin. *Ha! You'll feel better if the little boy goes to sleep.*

Tears rolled down his chubby cheeks, Logan let out a wail. "Nooo! No sleep." He pushed himself to a sitting position.

"Logan, this isn't open to discussion. You lay on that bed and take a nap."

"Nooo!" His weeping turned to wails.

Robyn put her hands on the boy's shoulder and pushed him back to a reclining position.

"Ahhh! No, no, no!" The boy kicked his feet into the air.

"Logan, you stop this right now."

He continued to wail and kick.

Horrified, Rosa watched as Robyn slapped the boy's face, then held his ankles to the bed.

She hurried across the room and touched her boss on the shoulder. "Miss Robyn, stop. You're scaring him."

"You deal with him, then. I've got work to do." Robyn released his feet and darted out of the room.

Rosa sat on the edge of the bed and took Logan's hand.

His wailing and thrashing turned to whimpering as he tried to control his sobbing hiccups. He stuck his thumb in his mouth.

"Don't cry, little one. I know you're scared and don't understand what's going on."

The little boy looked at her with wide eyes. "I want Mama."

Rosa cocked her head to one side. "You mean Miss Robyn? The lady with the red hair?"

Tears welled in the boy's eyes, and he shook his head. "*My* mama."

60

BROOKE

As Sugar drove Dazzle's SUV back to the ranch-style house in Reseda, Brooke's stomach rolled and gurgled and her heart pounded. The cargo compartment held, a playpen, disposable diapers, bottles, and toys for children of various ages. There were also bags of groceries.

But what if Dazzle didn't approve of the stuff they'd bought? Would he beat her? Worse yet, what if he found out Sugar had driven her to Victims of the Street before shopping?

It hadn't taken much to persuade the older girl, but Sugar had warned her what she could and couldn't say.

"Don't talk about us—about Daddy or me, or…none of it—you got it? I mean it! You can tell them you don't know where your sister is. Maybe they will know. I mean…I gave her a business card for this place, too. But, most importantly, tell them how to get ahold of your parents. Work with the lady on a plan to get you home. Let your parents try to find Candi."

Brooke had been disappointed when Sugar hadn't come inside with her.

She'd met with a woman named Araceli, but Brooke had gotten so nervous when the lady had tried to find out where she was staying and who else lived in the house, Brooke had made an excuse and run out of the building to the parking lot. She hadn't even told the woman her last name.

When she'd jerked open the passenger door, Sugar's eyebrows had arched in surprise. "That was fast. What happened?"

"They were asking about where I was staying and who lived there with me. I got nervous and ran out."

"Did they call your parents?"

"We didn't get that far."

Sugar wilted over the steering wheel and sighed. "I don't know if I'll ever be able to bring you back here. I can't keep protecting you from Dazzle…and the other girls. They're already mad that you get to watch kids and don't have to turn tricks."

"What does that mean?"

Pushing hair out of her face, Sugar shot her an incredulous look. "Look, you gotta grow up. We're prostitutes. We have sex with men who pay us. Dazzle is our leader. He's called a pimp. He's in charge of making all the arrangements.

"He's been pretty distracted these last few days, but I

can't protect you forever. He's going to want to turn you out soon, which means he'll have sex with you first, and then sell you to men who will make you do all kinds of things you don't want to do."

As the older girl had talked, tears had started to run down Brooke's face…not for the grim forecast of her own life, but knowing that her sister had already experienced the same dreadful acts.

As they pulled into the driveway of their house, Sugar gave her one last warning. "You can never tell Dazzle I took you to Victims of the Street. If you do, he'll kill both of us."

PART VII

61

———

AMBER

Amber and Roy hadn't said a word during the drive to Devonshire Station.

About a minute out, Amber broke the silence. "I don't think Duke would have us come to the station if they knew he was…gone." She picked at a hangnail on her thumb as her heart hammered. "I mean…they'd come to us to break the news. Right?"

Roy grunted, his face pale, his expression stony. "Then why didn't she say anything else?" He used his ID card to activate the security code, gaining them access to the employee parking lot, and swung his truck into an empty stall.

Walking with purpose, they hurried inside to the detective squad room.

As they entered, the routine drone of ringing phones

and conversations seemed to pause. Every detective watched them approach Duke at her desk.

"This isn't going to be good news," Roy mumbled.

Duke looked up from her paperwork, immediately rose, and moved to meet them. "Follow me. I've asked to use the captain's office. He's downtown at a meeting."

Amber exchanged a glance with Roy. He was right. Good news wasn't coming.

She escorted them into the administrative office and motioned toward some chairs. "Take a seat." Duke closed the door.

They wasted no time in taking a chair, and she followed suit.

"We may have a lead," she said.

Amber gasped. "What is it?"

"After we released the photo of Gage and the official press release, we got a call from a guy named Max O'Neil. Does that name mean anything to you?"

Roy shook his head. "No. Who is he?"

Duke looked at Amber. "Do you know him?"

"The name sounds familiar, but I don't think I know him. Should I?"

"Well," she looked at one of the papers in front of her, "He's an actor and stuntman. He called after seeing the news about Gage's kidnapping. He said that he was in the area of the kidnapping at the time it happened."

Amber leaned forward. "What did he see?"

Duke sighed and made a face. "Nothing. He was working. That accident you witnessed—the guy on the bike getting hit by a car? That accident was staged."

"What?" Amber felt her face warm.

"It was staged, an audition for a movie role for the two people involved. Max O'Neil was the driver of the car."

"*That's* why the name sounded familiar! I took his driver's license and gave it to the patrol unit."

"Who hired him?" Roy's tone was urgent.

"That's the problem. He won't tell us."

"Why not?"

"He and his buddy, the bicyclist and fellow stuntman, Greg Kendell, signed non-disclosure agreements. It was part of the audition."

"What the hell?" Amber blurted.

"Threaten to charge them both with making a false police report," Roy said.

"Or obstructing an investigation," Amber added.

Duke scoffed. "We can't get the DA to file charges on solid murder cases these days. No one will buy doing jail time for a weak misdemeanor."

Amber noticed Roy's jaw muscle clench.

"Let me talk to him. I'll get him to change his mind."

"No. Neither of you can be involved with the interviews," Duke said. "I've asked them to come in again. They should be here any minute."

Amber sat up straighter. "Well, we can watch."

Duke shook her head. "That's not a good idea."

Roy frowned. "Why not?"

Duke's expression hardened. "Because I don't want to jeopardize our case if these guys are involved. It's a courtesy that I told you about them at all."

"A courtesy? Our little boy has been missing for a day and a half, and you think it's a courtesy to tell us you have a lead?" Amber felt her cheeks warm. "You scare us to death, going through this cloak and dagger routine, just to tell us about some stunt men? I'm sure I should be more courteous, but I haven't seen a whole lot of progress in finding our boy."

Roy reached toward her. "Amb—"

Duke squared her shoulders. "I didn't have to tell you squat, *Officer* Buckner. You're here because I empathize with you and your husband. But if you're going to become a distraction to the investigation, then maybe you'd better go home…like any other parent whose child is missing."

Roy sighed. "Come on, Lavonne."

The lead detective turned to him and glared. "And that goes for you as well, *Detective.*"

Amber realized she and Roy *were* lucky to be so involved with the investigation and that they were dangerously close to losing the privilege. She softened her tone. "I'm sorry. Of course, we don't want to do anything that would undermine the investigation. But please…let us watch as you interview O'Neil and Kendell? Maybe they'll say something that could make sense only to us."

Roy, taking her lead, also spoke up. "We might think of a question to ask that doesn't occur to you."

The female detective took a deep breath, then exhaled. "There's no way I'm letting you sit in, but I will let you watch the interview on the monitor in the control room."

"Fine," Amber said. "Will you come check with us before you let them go…in case we have questions?"

Duke nodded. "I can do that." She rose from her chair. "I'll start with O'Neil since he contacted me first. There's not a lot of room in that control room, but you can set up a couple of chairs in case the interview goes on a while."

62

ANTONIO

As Antonio and his sister walked through the Victims of the Street offices, he pulled his car keys from his pocket. "Let's grab a late lunch, and you can tell me everything the little girl said."

Araceli sighed. "She wasn't here all that long. Maybe a half-hour, more or less. She was really skittish."

"I don't care. I want to know everything." He told his sister about meeting Candi early Sunday morning. "I want to keep looking for her. She was new to the street, and she'd be easier to convince to leave." He grinned. "Maybe we can rescue her and get her to leave her pimp."

Araceli scoffed. "I wouldn't get your hopes up. Pimps don't willingly let their girls leave."

They walked out into the hallway.

"I need to let Linda know I'm going out to lunch and on a possible field trip with you."

He nodded and smiled. "Now you're getting with the program."

Linda Tyler, the founder of Victims of the Streets, counted on his sister to help run the shelter and make the girls feel comfortable. Araceli was a living example of someone who'd been in the life and had gotten out and started over.

Araceli returned from Linda's office and left word with the young girl at the front desk. "I'll be back in a little while. Linda is in her office if you need anything."

Twenty minutes later, they sat outside a fast-food joint under an umbrella eating burgers and fries.

Araceli swallowed. "Tell me more about this Candi girl."

Antonio set down his soda and relayed his first encounter with Candi on San Fernando Road. "She could barely walk in the high-heeled boots she was in. She talked pretty tough for her first night, but I could tell she was new. I showed her your picture from when you were working the streets and told her you were my sister…that you'd gotten out of the life, and she could, too." He popped a french fry into his mouth. "She got freaked out, so I didn't push her. I did tell her about VoTS, and where you were located."

His sister nodded and took another bite of her burger.

He shook his head. "It sure doesn't take a pimp long to establish himself as the father-figure."

Araceli made a face. "Nope. The little girl said it all started when her sister got a secret boyfriend—some guy she met online and texted for a few weeks. When the sister was going to meet with him for the first time, Brooke insisted on tagging along, for safety. Araceli flashed him a look. "The boyfriend took them out to eat, and shopping for some new clothes…according to her, clothes their mother never would have bought them."

"Then what happened?"

"I don't know. I started asking questions about the boyfriend and she got scared and took off."

Antonio swallowed the last bite of his burger. "What do you say we go back to San Fernando Road and see if I can find Candi?"

His sister nodded. "It's pretty early, but okay. Let me hit the bathroom first." She rose from the table, unlocked her phone, and sat it next to him. "Check out the Spicy Bottoms app. It's a new site the pimps are using to advertise their girls. This one showed up after the personals on Adult Readers Today website got removed, this app showed up."

Antonio opened the app and was inundated with ad after ad of scantily clad young girls in provocative poses.

He narrowed the search to girls in the San Fernando Valley and jumped when the first picture on the screen was Candi.

His sister returned.

He showed the photo to her. "This is her. This is Candi."

She took the phone from him and examined the photo. "I'd be surprised if she was fifteen. Experienced pimps do photo shoots when they're first turned out, before the drugs age them about a decade every six months."

"I think I'll call and book a date with her. Looks like she's now doing in-call service as Jasmine."

"I'm surprised. There's a lot more chance of the pimp

getting popped by vice cops doing in-call." His sister made a face. "Of course, the pimp can charge more money and there's less chance of anyone getting arrested than on the street."

Antonio called the number listed on the app.

A male answered. "Hello."

"Yeah, I'm looking for a date. I saw Jasmine on Spicy Bottoms. Is she available?"

"She's available. When?"

"Depends. I'm in the Valley. Where are you?"

The male rattled off an address and the nearest major cross streets as Antonio scribbled the information on a napkin.

"Okay, bro, see you in a bit." He hung up and looked at Araceli. "I'm in."

"What's your game plan? Like I said, her pimp isn't exactly going to let you just walk out of there with his newest girl."

"I'll talk to her and try to get her to meet me at Victims of the Street when she can."

"He's moved his operation from the streets to in-call. It's going to be hard for her to get away."

Antonio shrugged. "Well, I've got to try." He threw away their trash and asked as they headed to his car, "Are you coming with me, or should I take you back to work?"

"You'd better take me back to work. You'll spook the pimp if he sees you show up with a girl in your car. Besides, maybe the little girl Brooke will show up again."

He looked at his sister intently. "If she does, do whatever it takes to make her stick around."

63

AMBER

On a monitor in the video control room, Amber and Roy watched Max O'Neil, his right leg bouncing with nervous energy, as he sat alone in interview room one.

Duke poked her head into the control room. "You guys all set?"

They both nodded.

"I've got the other guy, Kendell, waiting in the detective lobby. If they're involved in the kidnapping, he can worry about what O'Neil is telling us." Duke turned toward the door.

"Good luck," Amber said, as Duke started to shut the door.

"Thanks."

She and Roy watched as Duke and one of her senior detectives interviewed Max O'Neil.

First, she had the stuntman recount how he and Greg Kendell had been contacted by a casting director for an upcoming film.

"The director was looking for two guys who could pull off an auto-versus-bicycle stunt and make it look real. The casting director wouldn't tell us who was directing, but either way, this audition would provide an excellent video for our portfolios, and she assured us that we'd get a copy of the video within twenty-four hours of the audition."

Duke looked up from her notes she was taking. "How did you communicate with the casting director?"

"Strictly by phone—except when we met with her at her office to sign the papers."

"Where was her office?"

"Some place over by Universal Studios. I don't know the address, but I could show you where it is."

"Did you get the promised video?"

O'Neil's features hardened. "No. That's one reason why I'm here. Greg and I worked for ten days perfecting that accident. Neither one of us got what we were promised, except a two-hundred-dollar stipend—up front."

"Did you try calling the casting director afterward?"

"Yeah. We both did." O'Neil hung his head. "The number was no longer in service." He looked at Duke, his face filled with anguish. "It wasn't until I saw the news about that little boy being kidnapped that I thought maybe Greg and I were set up."

The detective bore his gaze into his. "So, why are you

honoring the casting director's NDA if you haven't received what you were promised?"

O'Neil shrugged.

"What's her name, Max?"

64

―――――

ROBYN

Robyn retreated to her office on the other side of the house. It wasn't the first time since she'd brought Logan home that she'd wondered if she'd done the right thing. What did she know about being a mother? How did she think she was going to be able to work while a toddler soaked up all her time and energy? *Yes, but once you've implemented your idea, things will be easier and fall into place.* Bolstered by her realization, she sat at her desk and thought about her next move as she doodled on a scratch pad. "Maybe, just maybe," she whispered, "I should take the next step. It's early, but I think necessary."

There was a light knock at the door.

Robyn frowned. Rosa rarely disturbed her when she was in her office. "Yes, Rosa. Come in."

The housekeeper opened the door with hesitance.

"Come in. It's okay." She motioned the other woman to sit in one of the upholstered chairs facing the desk.

Rosa took a seat. "I just wanted you to know that Logan is asleep. It only took a few minutes…once he calmed down."

That's right. Let me know that you're better with children than me. "Great. Thank you."

"Miss Robyn, may I ask you a question?"

"Sure."

"What happened to Logan's parents? How is it he was available for adoption?"

Keep calm. "It's my understanding that both of his parents were killed in a car accident." She shrugged. "I guess no other family members wanted him."

"Did he live in California, or did he come from another state."

Careful. Frowning, Robyn suppressed her uneasiness. "Why do you ask?"

It was the housekeeper's turn to shrug. "I'm just curious. He seems like such a sweet boy." She smiled. "You're lucky to have him."

"Yes. Yes, I am." She shuffled some papers on her desk. "With Logan asleep, is it time for you to leave?"

Rosa flinched. "Yes, of course, Miss Robyn. I just need to grab my purse." The maid hurried out of the office.

Robyn followed at a more leisurely pace and met Rosa, who had grabbed her belongings, by the front door. "I'll walk out with you. I want to get the mail."

The two walked down the front walk toward the street.

Next door, the gardeners—the same ones who serviced Robyn's yard—loaded equipment onto their truck.

She handed a check to the other woman. "Thank you for coming on such short notice."

"You're welcome. I'll see you next Thursday, as usual." Rosa took a few steps, then paused. "I, uh, wouldn't let the boy sleep too long, or you might have trouble getting him to sleep tonight."

"He's *my* son," she said, thumping her hand on her chest. "I know what to do for him!"

Rosa's eyes widened, and she took a few steps backward. "I'm sorry Miss Robyn. I didn't mean to imp—"

"The hell you didn't!" Robyn glanced at the gardeners pretending to secure their tools but eyeing the two women from beneath their wide-brimmed straw hats instead.

"All day you've hinted that I don't know how to take care of him. I'm a good mother. You don't know anything about how good I am with kids." She took pleasure in the house-keeper's shocked expression.

"I'm sorry, Miss Robyn. I'm sorry. I'll go now." Rosa lowered her head and raced toward the street.

"I expect to see you here on Thursday," Robyn yelled after her.

65

ROY

As soon as O'Neil revealed the casting director's name, Lori Heath, Roy checked various databases for information on the woman at an unmanned detective's desk.

He found several possibilities in the Los Angeles area, but he needed more information, to find the right Lori Heath.

He returned to the video control room.

Amber swiveled in her seat as he returned to the small space. "Did you find her?"

He shook his head. "There are too many. We'll need more info. What about a phone number?"

She nodded. "He had that in his phone. I've already called it, and like he said, it's no longer in service."

"Damn. That doesn't do us any good." He looked at her. "Do you even think she's a casting director?"

"I don't know. My guess is that it's not her real name. I mean, if you were going to go through this elaborate scheme in order to kidnap a kid, you're probably smart enough not to leave a trail straight back to you."

He frowned. "You know what this means, don't you? One of us was specifically targeted."

They watched as Duke finished up the interview with O'Neil and had the other detective walked the actor out to the lobby.

Duke leaned against the doorframe of the small control room, her notes in hand. "There's not much to go on. Did you run her already?"

Roy nodded. "There's a lot of Lori Heaths in LA. We've got a named suspect. Should we bring in SIS?"

"We're not even sure this Lori Heath is good info." Duke straightened her jacket. "I spoke to the chief earlier today, and I don't know what's going on, but he said SIS is tied up for at least a week."

Amber frowned. "They're too busy to work the kidnapping of an LAPD officer's son?" Her tone was incredulous.

Duke shrugged. "They must be working something huge…maybe terrorists. He *did* offer pretty much anything else we needed."

She glanced toward the detective lobby. "We're going to interview Kendell next. I've got O'Neil standing by. Afterward, we're going to drive the two of them over to Studio City to see if we can find the casting director's office."

Duke looked at both of them. "This is looking more and

more like a targeted kidnapping, not just a crime of opportunity. You two need to look at your own lives for anything or anyone who would want to hurt you. And the first thing to think about is who would know that Amber would have Gage in that location at that exact time."

66

———————

DAZZLE

With every passing minute, rage built in Dazzle.

Sugar and Kitty had been gone for almost two hours. He'd tried calling Sugar's cell phone, but he'd forgotten he'd taken it from her before they left.

Finally, he saw his SUV speeding down the street, then bouncing into the driveway.

He met them as they climbed from the vehicle. "Where the hell you been? You've been gone for hours."

Sugar gave him a warm smile. "I'm sorry, Daddy. Kitty picked out the perfect playpen, but they had to hunt to find the last one in their warehouse."

Kitty spoke. "I had a hard time choosing toys that would be good for both boys and girls."

You gave her a job and she's taking it seriously. Can't be mad at that. He glared, unwilling to let them think it was okay. "Get that shit in the house for now. I'm going to have to find a bigger house. I can't run the dating service and house kids here." He looked at Sugar. "Once the car's unloaded, get yourself pretty. I've got a john on his way. Eden's already working, and Diamond is just finishing up with a trick." He looked at Kitty. *Maybe it's time to show her what life is all about.* Something caught his eye in the front yard.

Diamond's john walked to his car parked on the street just as another car pulled up and parked behind it.

Must be the guy who called about Jasmine. "Sugar, I think your trick just arrived." *Breaking in Kitty will have to wait.* As he went inside, he glanced back at Sugar and Kitty. "You two get a move on."

67

____

ANTONIO

ntonio pulled up to a ranch-style house in Reseda just as another man walked across the grass toward a car parked at the curb.

He gave the guy a nod as he approached the house.

The other guy lowered his head, lengthened his strides, hopped in his car, and took off.

The front door opened, and a stocky, well-muscled dude greeted him. "Can I help you?"

"Yeah, I called earlier for a date with Jasmine."

The guy grinned and opened the screen door. "Come on in."

Antonio took in the feeble attempts at making a dumpy house look better.

"Have a seat," the man said. "What kind of date do you want?"

"Oral," he said, taking a seat in one of the folding chairs.

The other man nodded. "Fifty bucks."

"That's pretty steep, but Jasmine looks like she'll be worth it."

"I'm afraid that Jasmine isn't available. But I've got my best girl, Sugar, getting ready for you."

Antonio clenched his fists, but quickly relaxed them and forced himself to keep the frustration out of his voice. "I called and specifically booked *Jasmine*. The man I talked to said she was available."

"I understand, but she's not feeling well."

He rose. "Well, then I guess I'll head out." He started toward the door, then turned back. "You know, you're not going to stay in business very long if you bait and switch on your customers."

The man's eyes narrowed, and a muscle jumped in his jaw. "Tell you what I'm going to do…stud. I'm gonna give you a freebie with Sugar. Can't have you leaving my place unsatisfied."

Not willing to miss an opportunity of trying to talk a girl out of the life, Antonio nodded.

A few minutes later, a curvy girl of mixed descent entered the room. A satiny lavender robe tied tight around her waist. "Hi. I'm Sugar."

He sized her up as they walked down the hall. *She's been a working a while…* He spotted the ink—a crown tattooed on her wrist and a dollar sign on her neck, beneath her ponytail. *…had at least two pimps.*

She opened bedroom door and ushered him inside.

The room was dimly lit by two small lamps placed on a

dresser against the wall. A twin-sized mattress, box springs, and a single pillow sat in the middle of the room. There was space to walk completely around the bed.

Sugar smiled. "Why don't you get out of those clothes, and I can help you relax."

He glanced at the closed door. "I'm not here to have sex. I just want to talk to you."

The girl eyed him with suspicion. "I don't get paid to talk."

He sighed. "I'll pay you, but you should know your pimp gave you to me for free."

Sugar's brows furrowed. "Daz doesn't give anyone a free ride."

"I wanted to book Jasmine. I know her as Candi. Where is she?"

The girl stiffened. "I don't know anything about her." She shifted her weight back and forth. "I think you'd better go."

"I met her the other night, and I think she might be in trouble."

Sugar bit her lip and rolled her eyes.

She knows something.

The floor creaked in the hallway.

He lowered his voice to a whisper. "Look, I can help you get out of the life. There's a place called Victims of the Streets—"

"I know about it," she snapped, her tone also low.

"You don't have to sell yourself. I can make it so you *and* Candi, or whatever her name is, can get out of the game and be safe."

"I can't go back to a straight life, not ever. And you're too late for Candi."

"What do you mean?"

"Figure it out."

"She's dead?"

Sugar stared for several long seconds before finally speaking. "You got a card and a phone number? I might have someone you can help, but you'd have to pick her up."

Antonio pulled out a VoTS business card and wrote his cell number on the back. "Day or night," he said, handing her the card. "One other thing. You heard any talk of a pimp dealing in little kids? There's chatter about it on the street."

A look of surprise filled her face, and she shook her head vehemently.

Play it cool. "Well Sugar, take care of yourself, and call me. I can help you and any other girls who want out." He gave her two twenties and left.

68

———

ROSA

Rosa, heart pounding, scurried away from Robyn's house. As she passed the gardeners lingering by their truck, she lowered her head and averted her eyes.

The oldest man spoke to her in Spanish. "That lady's temper is as fiery as her hair."

Rosa paused, biting her lip, as tears rolled down her cheeks. She took a deep breath. "I was only trying to help. I'm so worried about the little boy."

The three men formed a semi-circle around her.

The older man's face lined with concern. "Who is the boy? Why do you worry?"

She shook her head. "Miss Robyn adopted him—at least, that's what she said. She doesn't know how to take care of him. She didn't even know how to put him down for a nap."

One of the younger gardeners, a guy she'd never seen before, tilted his head. "Do you think she is lying?"

Rosa eyed the guy's gang tattoos, knowing she had said too much. "I don't know. Maybe. It's just…she never said anything about wanting a child, and then, boom—suddenly there is a little boy living with her." She wiped her tears away and shrugged. "It doesn't make any sense."

The older man nodded. "Do you think you will continue to work for her?"

Rosa nodded. "Miss Robyn can be demanding, but this is the first time she's ever yelled at me like that. Normally, she is easy to work for and the pay is good. Everything about this feels wrong."

"I'm sorry. You are one of the few housekeepers who bring us snacks and water." The man chuckled. "We appreciate you…and thank you."

"You're welcome." She glanced at her watch. "I have to go, or I'll miss my bus and have to wait another hour for the next one."

As she hurried down the street, the older man called out, "Try not to worry, Rosa! Children are tough little creatures. The boy will be fine."

69

PAYTON

Payton considered the ways she could sneak out of the hospital all afternoon. Getting out of the building wouldn't be too hard. The biggest obstacle was the IV the doctors had inserted into her arm. She knew she didn't have the nerve to try and take it out herself, so until that needle was removed, she wasn't going anywhere.

Her night shift nurse came in to get her dinner tray. "Not the dinner of champions, huh?" She eyed the half-eaten roll and the untouched meatloaf.

Payton made a face. "No."

"Good news…we're going to take out your IV as soon as we get the dinner trays out of the rooms. You don't need it anymore."

"Really?" *Yes!* Her heart pumped with excitement.

"Yeah." The nurse stepped into the hallway, depositing

the tray onto a cart, and poked her head back into the room. "I'll be back just as soon as I can."

She couldn't hold back her grin. "Great." The moment the nurse was gone, she began planning her escape.

Earlier in her stay, one of her nurses explained that when family members visited patients in the ICU, they had to put on protective clothing, so she knew there was a cupboard in the hallway where hospital gowns, gloves, masks and booties were stored. Her best bet was to disguise herself as a hospital employee.

She'd wait until things quieted down in the hallway and pilfer a set of scrubs, a mask, and some booties.

She wasn't sure what she'd do once she got out of the hospital…but she knew if she had to, she could barter her body for a ride to the motel and get Brooke.

A while later, the nurse returned, with another young woman following her.

"Sorry it took me so long." The nurse motioned to the other woman. "This is Araceli Espinosa. She works at a local shelter for young women who don't have anywhere to stay." The nurse busied herself in removing the IV from Payton's arm.

Araceli moved to the side of the bed. "I work for a non-profit called Victims of the Streets. The hospital sometimes calls us when they have a patient being released without a place to go."

No! No! No! She couldn't go with this woman. She had to get her sister. "What if I don't want to go with you?"

The younger woman smiled slightly. "I'd ask you where you were planning to go."

"I have a boyfriend and friends I can stay with."

"And where do they live?"

"They rent a place on San Fernando Road."

"Ah, one of the flat back hotels." Araceli nodded. "I've been there and done that."

Payton clenched her teeth. "It's not like that."

The other woman's tone was non-confrontational. "If they were truly your friends, why haven't they visited you in the hospital?"

The nurse finished removing the IV and slipped out of the room.

"They probably didn't know where I was. I went on a date—"

"You have a boyfriend, and he lets you go out on dates with other men?"

Payton paused. "Um…sometimes."

Araceli pulled a chair next to the bed. "Look. Let's cut the BS. You've been working as a prostitute. Someone, probably your pimp, beat you up badly enough that you were taken to the hospital." She looked her up and down. "From the looks of you, you haven't been tricking too long." Araceli smiled at her. "I've been there…for years. I was addicted to drugs, raped numerous times, which led to all kinds of STDs, and almost murdered." She tilted her head. "Is that the life you want to lead?"

Payton couldn't look at her.

Araceli whispered. "Where are you from?"

"Nowhere," she said, softly.

"I'm sure your family is worried sick about you."

She scoffed. "Not anymore. I've sinned. I'm ruined."

The woman took her hand. "Trust me. No matter what you've done, your family wants you back."

She shook her head and tears slid down her cheeks. "No, they won't. My boyfriend said so."

"Of *course* he did. He's making money off you. Why would he want you going back to your former life? He has everything to gain if you believe what he's told you and go back to him. What do you get? A hard life and an early grave?"

"I can't go home. Not yet."

"Why not?"

"He's got something of mine, and I have to get it back."

70

AMBER

Roy and Amber followed the older gold Crown Vic, driven by Duke along with one of her detectives riding shotgun, and O'Neil and Kendell in the backseat.

Amber looked at Roy as they pulled onto the Golden State Freeway. "Do you think we'll find the office where they met with Lori Heath…or whoever it was?"

He nodded. "I think so. O'Neil definitely seemed like he wanted to help."

The detective car turned into the driveway of a small strip mall containing a nail salon, a flower shop, and a donut shop.

Duke parked the sedan with the detectives and witnesses parked in front of an empty storefront next to the flower shop, and Roy pulled his truck into a space facing Cahuenga Boulevard.

The group gathered in front of the empty storefront.

"Yeah, this is where we met Lori Heath," O'Neil was saying.

Duke peered through the glass of the front window. "There's nothing in there now." She tried the door, but it was locked.

"What kind of furniture did she have in there?"

Kendell glanced at O'Neil. "A card table and a couple of chairs, right?" He looked at the detectives. "We thought it was weird, but she said she'd just leased the property."

O'Neil nodded. "She told us that's why she didn't have any business cards. She hadn't had time to get them made."

Roy crossed his arms. "And none of this seemed odd or suspicious to you?"

"She gave each of us two hundred dollars, man. Frankly, I needed the two bills more than the video of the stunt." Kendell shrugged.

Amber looked at Roy. "Why don't we check with the other shop owners."

Roy nodded and looked at Duke. "Do you want to contact Communications? They'll transfer you to the fire department's dispatch and get you the name of whoever owns this strip mall from the business permits."

Duke nodded. "Yeah, we'll do that while you guys hit the businesses." She looked at the two actors. "It sounds like it's going to take a long time, but it won't."

Amber and Roy strode down the front walkway and into the flower shop.

A middle-aged woman working on a flower arrangement smiled as they came in. "Hi there. May I help you?"

Amber smiled back. "Yes, but probably not in the way you mean." She showed the woman her ID card. "We're with the LAPD, and we were wondering if you could tell us about the last tenant that was in the building next door?"

The woman's eyebrows shot up and she grinned. "The cigar store? What's to tell? They picked a terrible location. I'm sure they thought they'd get all kinds of young people heading to Universal Studios to stop in and buy cigars before they hit the CityWalk, but for the most part, at least with the kids, smoking cigars was a short-lived fad."

Amber tucked her hair behind her ear. "Actually, we were talking about the female casting director. It probably looked like a business office when she leased the place."

The florist shook her head. "I'm sorry, but the only business that's been in that space in the last year was the cigar shop…and I've been here for ten years."

Amber looked at Roy.

"Do you have any security cameras, and if so, how long do you keep your videos?"

"I do, and they're stored in the cloud for two weeks."

"Damn it," Amber whispered. "This would have been about three weeks ago." She sighed. "You've never seen a woman in that space after the cigar shop closed?"

The woman shook her head. "I'm sorry, no."

Roy nodded. "Thank you for your time, Ma'am."

"Yes, thank very much," Amber said.

The woman's voice stopped them just as they were about to leave.

"If you don't mind me asking, what's this all about?"

"We're trying to track down a kidnapper."

"Oh, is it that cute little boy I've seen on TV? I hope you find him."

"So do we," they said in unison.

PART VIII

71

ROBYN

Robyn took another sip of her third martini. After her blow up with Rosa, she needed to calm down, and a classic martini was her go-to calming beverage. Even when working with brain-dead actors, directors, and producers, she rarely lost her cool in public.

Logan sat at the table; his face expressionless.

"Why aren't you eating your dinner? Don't you like it?"

Not moving his head, the boy looked at her.

Her heart sank. His eyes were filled with apprehension… and fear.

"Logan, honey, Mommy doesn't want you to be sad or scared. If you don't like sushi, I'll make you something else. What would you like?"

The child eyed her, uncertainty playing across his face.

Mellowed from the booze, she tried to encourage him. "What is it? What do you want to eat?"

His voice was barely a whisper. "Chicken nuggets an' french fries—with k-chup."

She fought the urge to roll her eyes. "Hmm, Mommy doesn't have that here."

His face crumbled.

"But…" she smiled. "I can have someone bring it to us. Would you like that?"

A hint of a smile tugged at the corners of his mouth, and he nodded.

"Would you like me to order the meal that comes with a toy?"

She was rewarded with a genuine smile and an enthusiastic nod. "Okay." She phoned in an order with a food delivery service. She even ordered a burger and medium fries for herself. "Must be the alcohol," she mumbled while mentally counting the calories, carbs, and fat content of her meal.

She led him to his room, she sat on the floor, and they played with building blocks until their dinner arrived.

Back at the kitchen table, she watched him stuff one fry after another into his mouth. "Don't forget the nuggets."

He nodded and dipped a piece of chicken into the ketchup she'd put on his plate.

She'd forgotten how delicious fast food tasted, and shamelessly wolfed it down as a kids show played in the background.

She was glad to see him eating so well. There was less chance of any problems with the larger dose of sleep aid she planned to give him before bedtime. Tomorrow was a big day, and she needed a solid night of rest to implement the second part of her plan so she could gain some relief.

She grinned at the idea. *Come tomorrow, everyone's life will be brighter.*

72

ROY

As Amber and Roy left the florist shop, Duke called out.

"Hey, guys, the fire dispatch said it'll take them a few minutes to get me the strip mall owner's information." She joined them on the sidewalk. "Did the flower shop have any info?"

He shook his head and repeated what the florist had told them.

"I don't see any point in sticking around. We got what we came for—the address for." Duke looked at the two actors. "We'll get you back to the station."

"Before we leave, Lavonne, why don't you and I walk around the back? Just in case we can get inside…" Roy focused his gaze on hers, hoping she'd understand there was more than a potentially unlocked door on his mind.

She nodded, then glanced at the other detective and Amber. "We'll be right back." As soon as they were out of earshot, she spoke. "Okay. What's up?"

"I could be totally wrong, but what you said about the kidnapping being targeted toward me or Amber got me to thinking."

"And?"

"Right after Amber and I separated, I had a few…dates with a woman I'd met during the Justin Lowe case. She's a casting director."

They rounded the side of the strip mall and Duke stopped, placing her hands on her hips. "And you're just telling me this now?"

"It's the first opportunity I've had."

"What's this woman's name, and why would she kidnap your son?"

"I'm not saying she's kidnapped Gage, but it *is* pretty strange that our first solid lead involves a casting director. Here name is Robyn McGee, and there's absolutely no reason for her to snatch Gage. I haven't seen her in over a year."

They resumed walking along the back wall of the businesses.

"If you were separated, what's the big deal about Amber knowing you were dating?"

He shrugged. "I don't know. It was just weeks after Amber walked out. It might hurt her."

The detective scoffed. "You guys need a good therapist. Do you know where this McGee woman lives?"

Roy felt his face warm. "In Bel Air."

"Do you have the address?"

"I could find the house."

"Does McGee know where you live and that you have a son?"

He nodded. "Yeah, she does."

They reached the rear door of the empty store in the strip mall.

Roy tried the door, and as they both expected, it was locked.

"Are you going to tell your wife about your relationship with McGee, or are you going to make me break that news?"

They turned back toward the front building.

"I'm telling you privately, so you can take a look at Robyn. If it turns out she's not involved, Amber never needs to know about her."

"And if she *is* involved?"

"I'll never forgive myself." He shook his head. "Amber never will either."

Returning to Devonshire Station, Roy and Amber once again followed the detective sedan into the parking lot.

"I'm going to hit the head," Amber said.

"Okay, meet me and Duke in the squad room."

She nodded as she headed down the hallway toward the restroom.

Duke joined Roy as her partner led O'Neil and Kendell back inside the station.

"I'm going to make up a six-pack, including Robyn McGee, and see if the actors can ID her."

"Well, do me a favor," Roy said. "I'll keep Amber busy while you do the photo line-up. If they don't recognize Robyn, Amber doesn't have to know."

Duke sighed and shook her head as she walked toward the detective squad room.

When Amber came out of the bathroom, Roy motioned to her. "Duke asked us to get her some decent coffee. Apparently, the machine in the detective squad room is broken, and she won't drink patrol coffee."

"Tell her to get her own coffee. We need to find Gage."

"Come on. It will only take a few minutes, and I wouldn't mind a good cup myself."

"Fine. But let's make it snappy."

Twenty minutes later, when they returned, Duke pulled him aside.

"I've got bad news. The owner of the strip mall hasn't rented out his building to a casting director—or anyone else, for that matter— since the cigar store."

"Then how did Lori Heath get inside?"

"Turns out, the owner *lent* the space to his good friend *Robyn McGee* to run some auditions."

"Oh, shit."

"She told him it was a last-minute casting call, and she had nowhere else to hold the amount of people she was expecting."

"And I suppose the actors identified Robyn in the six-pack?"

Duke nodded and looked across the squad room where Amber was giving Duke's partner a cup of dark roast. I'll run a rap sheet and DMV record to get McGee's address. You need to tell your wife. Do you want to use the captain's office? I can have the janitor let you in."

Amber sauntered up to them. "Did the fire department call back yet?"

"We were just discussing it. I've got some things to check out." Duke smiled. "Roy, why don't you tell Amber what we've learned." Duke headed toward her desk and logged into her computer.

Amber's face had paled. "What is it? Why is she acting weird, and why do you look like you want to puke?"

"Let's go out to the car."

"Why? What's wrong. Is it Gage? Is he—"

"No. I don't have any news about Gage. But something has come up in the investigation and I need to tell you about it."

Amber's cheeks flushed, her breathing increased, and her lips formed a thin line. "Well, stop jerking me around and tell me."

He glanced around the squad room. In addition to Duke, there were some gang detectives sitting at their desks, and the night watch detective talking to a pair of patrol officers about an arrest they'd made. "Let's go outside where we have some privacy."

"Fine." Amber turned on her heel and marched to the station's rear exit, slamming her hands on the bar of the door release.

Once outside, she turned to him. "What the hell is going on?" Her face contorted with anger…and fear.

He took a deep breath. "Duke talked to the owner of the strip mall. He loaned that location to a friend of his who really is a casting director."

"Let me guess. Lori Heath?"

"No, a woman named Robyn McGee." He cleared his throat. "I know her. After you and I split up, I dated her for a couple of weeks."

73

———————

BROOKE

Brooke stored the toys she and Sugar had bought that morning in Dazzles bedroom. She listened to the news playing low in the background as she worked, hoping there might be a story about her and Payton missing from Idaho.

She realized she'd made a mistake by not trusting the nice lady at the victim's shelter. Maybe the police would have found Payton by now if she had been honest with her. She'd probably lost her chance.

When they were shopping, she'd shown Sugar both cards from Victims of the Street, the one Sugar had given to Payton, and the card Brooke had gotten from Araceli.

Sugar had demanded both, then pulled into a gas station, tore them into tiny pieces, and thrown them into the trash.

Brooke knew she needed to find another way to get to the Victims of the Street again. She didn't think Sugar would take her, especially since the older girl was scared to death that Dazzle was going to find out about their previous visit. Besides, there was no time.

Dazzle was excited by how busy the girls were staying. Driven by the money, Brooke knew he'd start looking to recruit some new girls.

He'd left Sugar in charge, booking dates on a burner phone.

When Sugar was busy with a client, Brooke filled in on the phone. The older girl tried to keep herself free and not leave her alone to handle things.

Sugar had already turned down one date and was in the process of turning down another when her cell rang.

She quickly booked the trick with Eden, then answered her personal cell. "Hi, Daddy. Is everything okay?"

Even though the phone wasn't on speaker, Brooke could hear Dazzle's voice clearly.

"Yeah, fine. How are things there?"

"Real good. We've been booking solid since you left."

"Don't book anything after two. We're going to be busy tomorrow."

Sugar frowned. "Okay, Daddy."

"I'll be back later tonight and should have two more girls with me."

Sugar stuck out her tongue but kept her voice light-hearted. "Great. We'll see you then. You know I love you, Daddy."

"Don't worry, babe. You're still my best girl. Talk to ya soon."

Sugar ended the call.

"What do you think we'll be doing tomorrow?" Brooke asked.

"I don't know, but I'm pretty sure we're not going to like it."

74

ROBYN

Robyn pulled Logan out of the bathtub, and her insides constricted as she wrapped him in a towel and caught a whiff of the clean little boy.

Not for the first time, she wondered if she'd made a mistake by putting her Hollywood career first. Even when she'd married Brent McGee, she'd told him that she didn't have time for children.

"They can come in a few years," she'd announced, without fear.

The problem was that "few" had turned into seven and she and Brent had divorced by then. By that time, she had long past her prime for bearing children.

But this little boy was the key to her finally having that family.

After placing him in a pull-on diaper and pajamas, she

got him into bed and handed him a sippy cup of chocolate milk. "You drink and I'll read you a story, okay?" She watched as he took his first taste.

Of course, the drink was laced with the liquid sleeping aid, but she'd added extra chocolate so he wouldn't notice.

When he settled back on his pillow, she began reading a story about a dinosaur that went to school.

Before she was halfway through the book, he was sound asleep.

She situated the covers over him and kissed him on the forehead. "Tomorrow will be a happy day, Logan. I promise." Walking down the hallway to her bedroom, she had to reach out a couple of times to balance herself and giggled each time. "Robyn, I do believe you've had too much to drink." She closed her bedroom door and went to a small wet bar against the far wall. "One more won't hurt. I probably won't even finish it once I start reading that new script." After shaking the vodka and vermouth with ice, she poured the mixture into a martini glass and pulled out the small jar of olives from the mini fridge. "Damn." It was empty. A martini isn't complete without the olives." She made her way back to the kitchen where she was hit with the greasy odor of Logan's leftover french fries.

Frowning at the waxy wrappers from their dinner scattered across the table, she scooped everything into a paper ball. *This crap will stink up the house.* She wobbled out to the garage to dispose of the wrappings in the garbage bin, but…"Where the hell are my garbage cans?" She yelled in frustration.

Sobering a little in her agitation, she marched toward

the pedestrian garage door that led to the backyard. Two trash barrels sat outside on the cement near the door.

She lifted the lid of the closest one, threw the trash in, and slammed the lid closed.

Returning to the kitchen, she found a new jar of olives in the pantry and took it back to the bedroom to top off her martini properly.

Swaying a bit, she set the drink on the nightstand, climbed into bed, picked up the script and began reading.

She couldn't focus on the words. She took another sip and admitted that she didn't feel like reading. Tossing the script away, she grabbed the TV remote instead, and tuned to the year's best film…unfortunately, not a film she'd cast. Sipping her martini, she imagined who she would have suggested to play the leads.

Soon, her eyelids drooped heavy, so she turned off the television and sank into a deep sleep.

75

AMBER

"What the hell have you done?" Amber stared at Roy. "You brought some psycho into our lives and now she's taken our son!" She lifted her arms and shoved him as hard as she could.

Roy stumbled back a couple of steps. "Amber, calm down. You're at a police station. There's video all over the place, and the last thing you want to do is get arrested for domestic abuse."

"You *asshole*! You bring this crap into our family and you threaten *me* with arrest?"

He held up his hands. "I don't know that she has Gage. But I doubt it's a coincidence. You need to calm down so we can find out what's going on."

"Fine. Let's go over to your girlfriend's house and find our son." She turned to go to his truck.

He grabbed her arm.

"Let go of me!"

"We can't do this—at least, not by ourselves. This is Duke's investigation and we're going to have to play by her rules."

Amber glared at Roy. She knew he was right, but his dating life had put their son in danger. She just knew it. "All right. Let's go in and get Duke's ass in gear. I want to go get our son."

"Look, I know you're mad at me, and that's fine. But you can't go charging in there, balls to the wall, and start ordering a D-3 around."

"Well, I'm not going to sit around wringing my hands or clutching my pearls. You ought to know me better than that."

"I *do* know you better than that." He gave her a small smile. "Let's see what Duke has come up with and we'll go from there. But remember, she gets to run the show."

Amber used her ID card on the door keypad to get them back into the station.

Roy nodded at Duke, and the detective walked out of her cubicle to meet them.

"Okay." She looked at Amber. "I guess you've been brought up to date."

Amber gave her a curt nod.

"I've found absolutely nothing indicating that Robyn McGee is our

kidnapper. She's never even had a speeding ticket." The detective handed a computer printout to Roy. "Is that the address you're familiar with?"

He scanned the paper. "Yes. What's our next move?"

"There is no next move for you *or* Amber. At this point, we're going to continue our investigation without your assistance."

Amber opened her mouth, ready to object, but Roy put his hand on her forearm.

"What is your plan?"

"My partner and I will go talk to McGee. Find out where she was on Monday morning and if she has an alibi."

"She doesn't have to talk to you, and you don't have enough for a search warrant," Amber said. "All we have is the fact she borrowed a friend's building to meet with some actors. There is *nothing* to place her at the kidnapping scene. In fact, the video showed my son being led away by a man."

Duke's features softened. "I know you're upset and worried, but you have to let us do our job."

Roy removed his hand from Amber's arm. "Let me go with you. Let me talk to her. We'll tell her that we talked to the actors, and we're hoping she has the video from their stunt. Maybe the kidnapping suspect was caught during the filming. We might get a chance to look around, or if Gage is there, he might hear my voice and call out."

"If you're going, I'm going," Amber said. "I'll ask to use the restroom and look around for him."

Duke frowned. "This investigation is going off the rails. The more people involved, the more likely something will go wrong. I don't want to lose any evidence from an illegal search."

"Lavonne," Roy said, "I think she'll be more likely to let us in if I'm there."

Amber was about to make a snide remark, but held her tongue. She needed access to Robyn McGee's house to find her son, and if she appeared to be emotional, they wouldn't take her along—and that wasn't going to happen.

76

PAYTON

It had taken almost two hours to get discharged from the hospital. The whole time, Araceli had talked about a lot of things, but her questions skirted around Payton revealing her name, and why she needed to go back to her pimp.

She was afraid to answer. What if she said something, and the police stormed into the motel, and there was a shootout, and Brooke was killed?

Dazzle had told her he had people inside of the police department, and he'd know if any of the girls were talking about him to cops.

Knowing how badly he'd beaten her, she didn't want to expose her sister to the same treatment.

Araceli had finally stopped asking questions as they drove to the Victims of the Street shelter.

Once inside, they went to Araceli's office, where the older girl pulled some papers out of a filing cabinet. She handed the paperwork and a pen to her.

"Go ahead and start filling this out. If you have any questions, just ask."

Payton nodded.

"Do you want to call your parents and let them know you're okay? We can do that right now if you want."

Her stomach tightened at the mention of her parents. "No, not yet." Tears filled her eyes as she looked at the young counselor. "How could I call and tell them *I'm* okay, but I don't have a clue where my sister, Brooke is or what's happened to her?"

Araceli's eyes widened. "Your sister's name is Brooke? Is your name Payton?" A grin filled Araceli's face. "Your sister was here earlier today. I talked to her."

77

ROY

Roy was exhausted. Between trying to help Duke in any way he could, and impeding Amber from taking her anger and frustration out on the lead detective, it seemed every clue ran them into the largest wall possible. He was running on empty.

As he knew it would, the investigation got bogged down in a flurry of phone calls up the food chain of the department brass.

Duke hung up her phone and shook her head.

Amber, pacing nearby, stepped to Duke's desk and looked down at her. "Well? What's happening? Has anyone made a decision?"

Roy came to stand next to Amber.

"These guys take all the tests and promote, but when the shit hits the fan and action needs to be taken, the pucker factor is too much for them." Duke sighed. "I'm waiting for a call from the chief."

Amber crossed her arms. "You know what? I don't have to wait. There's a possibility this McGee woman has my son. I'm going over there and get in that house one way or another."

"Amber," Roy warned, "talk like that is not helping."

She turned as quickly on him as the targets did on the firearms qualification course. "You have no right to criticize me. This is all your fault. If you'd kept your dick in your pants, this nut job wouldn't have our son."

Duke leaped from her chair. "Officer Buckner, you'd better rein it in. You're here because of my compassion for your situation."

The phone on Duke's desk rang, and she snatched the receiver. "Duke." She listened. "Yes, chief. I understand… yes, sir." She glanced at Roy first, then at Amber. "Yes, sir." Duke hung up and exhaled a heavy sigh. "Okay. We're good to go. He likes the idea of gaining access on the pretense of obtaining any video taken at the accident scene. If we can get a consent search, fine. She'll have to sign a consent search waiver. Otherwise, we're to back out and get enough evidence for a search warrant."

Duke pointed at Roy. "I'm counting on you to persuade her to let us take a look around."

He scoffed. "I don't guarantee anything. Since we think she may have Gage, things clearly didn't end as well as I thought they did."

Amber glared at him. "You think?"

The lead detective turned on Amber. "If you want to be included, you need to tamp down your anger. I don't want you tipping off McGee that she's a suspect, so keep your smart-ass remarks and dirty looks to yourself." Duke looked at her partner. "We're taking a black-and-white with us, just in case, but keep them down the street."

Duke's partner nodded. "I'll have the watch commander get us a unit."

Amber smashed her right fist into her left palm. "Well, come on, let's go!"

Duke placed her hand on Amber's shoulder. "Take a breath. Once the black-and-white is assigned, we'll fill them in and head out."

Amber shifted away from the detective's hand. "Get them on the radio, tell them where to meet us, and brief them there. We're wasting time." She turned on her heel and marched out of the squad room.

78

ANTONIO

Antonio's boss from the car sales lot called as he drove away from the brothel. It wasn't often that the boss asked him to do something extra, so when he did, Antonio was happy to help.

The task was simple enough: drive one of the cars from the car lot to Reno. A car broker in Nevada had an interested client. Rather than wait for a commercial vehicle transport, the broker wanted the car driven up overnight. He wouldn't arrive in Reno until about 3:00 am, but he'd been given enough cash to nap in a cheap motel for a few hours. His boss had booked him a morning flight back to Los Angeles.

Fortified with coffee and a cooler full of energy drinks, Antonio sped through the high desert west of Death Valley.

As he cruised up Highway 395, he marveled at the

number of stars visible when away from the bright city lights —the sky hovered like a blanket of black satin covered in silver glitter.

The ringing of his cell phone jarred his solitude, and he glanced at his screen before answering. "What's up, Celi?"

"You're not going to believe it. I've got Candi sitting right here in my office."

"What? How?"

"She's been in the hospital. Her true name is Payton, and she was beaten up by her pimp. The hospital called Victims of the Street because they needed the bed, and she was well enough to leave."

"That's awesome."

"There's more."

His heart pounded, but he said nothing.

"She's the sister of the little girl, Brooke, who came here and talked to me this morning."

"Is Brooke with her?"

"No. That's where you come in. We need to go get Brooke. Payton thinks she can find her way back to the motel on San Fernando Road."

"Celi, she's not there anymore, remember? The pimp moved his operation to the house in Reseda."

"Well, come get us. We'll call the police, and we can all go get Brooke."

Antonio chuckled. "That's not how it works. We need to be sure the kid is at that location. I didn't see any sign of her when I was there this afternoon."

"Then can you at least book an appointment for tonight?

"I would, but I'm on my way to Reno with a car."

"Oh, no. Why tonight of all nights?"

"I'll be back tomorrow, before noon. In the meantime, get Cand—Payton settled at the shelter. Find out if she knows anything about her pimp or anyone else dealing in little kids."

"Do you think I should try contacting the police?"

Normally, he'd call his buddy Roy, but with his son missing, he didn't want to bother his friend. "Not yet. Let me get back to LA and see what I can find out. If we see Brooke, we'll call in for reinforcements."

"Okay. Call me when your flight lands. I'll pick you up."

79

ROBYN

Robyn moaned and pulled her pillow over her head. Someone was pounding on something nearby. Even with the buffer covering her ears, the noise continued.

Then, the melodic ring of her doorbell caused her to toss the pillow aside and look at the clock on her nightstand. Almost midnight.

Who the hell would be at my door at this hour? Adrenaline kicked in and her heart raced as she found a robe, picked up her cell phone, and considered calling the Bel Air Security, but the pounding on the door started again.

Whoever was at the door was going to wake Logan.

For the first time in her life, Robyn wished she owned a gun. *Don't be silly. You wouldn't even know how to use it.* As a precautionary measure, she punched the Bel Air security number into her phone. If she didn't know the person at the door, she'd place the call. She knew the private security officers would be there long before the LAPD officers from West LA station could get to her home.

Tiptoeing to the heavy wooden front door, she looked through the peephole and gasped. *What was Roy Buckner doing here?* She needed to stall and think. "Who is it?"

"Robyn, it's Roy Buckner. Remember me? We met during the investigation of Justin Lowe."

"What do you want?" She felt her body sway. *Shit. You're still drunk.*

"Can you please open your door? I need to talk to you. It's official business. I have Detective Duke with me, as well as another female officer."

What to do? What to do? She unlocked the door, opened it a crack, and peered at the people on her porch. "It's awfully late. Can't it wait until tomorrow?"

A weary-looking woman in a gray pantsuit stepped forward. "Ms. McGee, I'm Detective Lavonne Duke from Devonshire Division, LAPD. Could we come in and talk to you? It's urgent."

If they knew anything, they'd have SWAT breaking down the door. She frowned and glanced out at the street, where everything appeared normal and quiet. But when she pulled the door open wider, she saw another woman and recognized her. Amber Buckner. Roy's wife.

Her heart raced as she allowed the trio inside, and led them to her family room, flipping on lights along the way. "I'm sorry. I'm a little foggy headed. You got me out of bed. Won't you please have a seat and tell me what this is all about?"

The two women sat in the wingback chairs next to the fireplace, while Roy took a seat on the sofa.

Robyn sat on the other end of the couch and looked at Roy.

"Have you seen the news about my son being kidnapped?"

"Yes. Yes, I did. I'm so sorry. I meant to call you, but I've just been so busy…"

Roy nodded. "It's fine. Actually, we're here because we spoke to some actors you auditioned for a part. We need some information."

Robyn willed her hands to stop trembling and thanked God her robe concealed her traitorous, quivering knees. "I'm afraid you'll have to be more specific. I audition dozens of actors in a week." She smiled at her former lover.

Amber Buckner leaned forward. "Max O'Neil and Greg Kendell. You hired them to do a vehicle-versus-bicycle stunt collision. You were supposed to have someone there taping the accident as an audition."

Seeing the intensity on the other woman's face, Robyn swallowed. "Oh, yes, I do remember that job."

Detective Duke smiled. "That's why we're here. We were wondering if we could obtain a copy of the stunt. You see, the Buckner boy was kidnapped right around that time near that location. We might get lucky and have video of the kidnapper."

Think, Robyn, think! "Then you came all this way for nothing. I was using a new cameraman and he screwed up. He failed to record the stunt. That's why I haven't sent the video to the actors." She gave a sheepish smile. "I hate delivering bad news."

Roy smiled. "Were you at the shoot? Maybe you saw something that might help us."

"No, I wasn't there. I was at court for the Lowe trial, remember? We were getting coffee together when you got the call about your son."

Amber rose. "Speaking of coffee…it goes right through me. May I use your bathroom?"

Robyn nodded. "There's a powder room next to the library, which is right off the front foyer."

"Thank you." Amber glanced at Roy. "I'll be right back."

"You have a lovely home," Duke said.

"Thank you so much. I'm comfortable here."

Roy rubbed his hands together. "How long have you lived here?"

"I think I told you when we were dating…almost twelve years."

Duke stood and walked around the room. "I just love the color palette you've used. The light creme with the vibrant red. It's very striking." The detective turned and gave her a bright smile. "Would you mind if I took a peek at your kitchen? Frankly, this is one of the nicest homes I've ever seen."

Robyn's stomach gurgled. *You need to get out of here.* There was an undercurrent of tension in the air. "Of course." She rose and led the way, turning on the hanging light fixtures over the massive kitchen island. *You're about to be sick.* Beads of sweat sprouted on her forehead and upper lip. "Would you excuse me for a minute?" Without waiting for an answer, she turned and left Duke and Roy in the kitchen.

She dashed through the master bedroom and into her

marble-fitted bath. *They're on to you.* She made it to the toilet just before her stomach rid itself of its contents. *Get them out of here. Tomorrow you can fix this. Not the way you intended, but it's better than them finding the boy here tonight.* Once her retching stopped, she quickly brushed her teeth and ran a cold washcloth over her face.

"Robyn? Are you all right?" Roy's voice grew louder as he moved closer to her bedroom.

Oh, no

"Ms. McGee?" Duke sounded as though she was right on Roy's heels. "Where are you?"

Robyn strode across the bedroom and out to the hallway.

Roy was coming toward her, while Duke opened the door to the guest room and flipped on the light, then turned it off and closed the door. Amber was opening the door to Logan's room.

"Wait! You've got no right to go in there."

Ignoring her, Amber opened the door and turned on the light.

Robyn stood frozen with the weight of what was coming.

"Roy, you need to come here," Amber called.

Robyn's heart threatened to burst through her chest when Roy grabbed her arm and pulled her along with him.

Duke followed behind them.

They entered Logan's train bedroom, but the bed was empty.

80

AMBER

Amber stormed into the room, looking behind furniture and marauding through the walk-in closet. "Where is he?" Coming up empty, she even checked the hamper and peeked inside the toy box. Her anger and panic rose with her every move.

Spotting Roy holding McGee by the arm, Amber advanced, her gaze fixed on the other woman's eyes. "What have you done with my son?"

The redhead shrugged to get out of Roy's grasp, but he held her tight and placed himself between the two. "Amber. Calm down."

"I won't calm down! That bitch took our son and now she's hidden him. I'm going to tear up this house room-by-room and find him."

Duke stepped forward. "No, we're not going to do that."

Amber couldn't get past Roy, McGee, and Duke all gathered at the entrance to the bedroom, so she shouted, "Gage! It's Mommy. Come out from wherever you're hiding."

Duke looked at McGee. "Do you have the Buckner boy? If you do, you need to tell us. It will go easier for you."

Amber stopped pacing and watched McGee.

The casting director lifted her chin. "I don't know what you're talking about."

"Yeah, right," Amber motioned toward the elaborate unmade bed. "You're big into trains, are you?"

Robyn displayed a saccharin smile. "This is where my nephew stays when he visits."

Duke moved so she could see McGee's face. "Is your nephew here now?"

"Do you see him?" Her tone was no longer helpful.

"When was the last time he visited?" Roy asked.

"This past weekend. My housekeeper hasn't been here yet to wash the sheets."

Duke motioned to Roy to release the redhead's arm. "Ms. McGee, would you give us permission to search your house?"

"Search for what? I don't understand what's going on. You came here looking for a video, and the next thing I know, I'm being manhandled and half the LAPD is poking their noses into private areas of my home—without a search warrant, I might add."

Roy released the casting director's arm and gave her a relaxed smile. "Robyn, just let us take a quick look around and then we'll get out of your hair."

"I don't think so. I haven't done anything wrong. I hired

some actors for a stunt—that's all. It's what I do. I'm sorry I don't have the video you're looking for. I would give it to you if I could." She pulled her robe more tightly around her body. "I think you all should leave now. If you want anything else from me, you can contact my attorney, Charmaine Baker. She's in Beverly Hills." The casting director pointed toward the hallway.

Duke squared her shoulders and exited the room.

Roy waited for Amber at the bedroom door.

As she walked past the redhead, she whispered, "This isn't over." She called out with every step she took. "Gage! Gage! It's mommy. Please come out."

PART IX

81

ROY

As Duke's partner drove through the exit gates of Bel Air, Duke filled him in as to what had happened inside. Although everything pointed to a child having recently been in the house, there was no sign of Gage Buckner anywhere.

"While I was covering the backyard, I noticed the pedestrian door to the garage was wide open. There were two trash bins outside the door. I took a quick peek but didn't see anything of interest in there—just some fast-food wrappers, grass cuttings, and a curtain or something," the partner said.

Roy felt the anger radiating off of Amber in waves from the other side of the sedan's backseat. "You know damn well that Gage was in that house. There *must* be a way we can get a search warrant," she said, glaring at him.

He shook his head. "We don't have enough probable

cause. But Robyn was right about one thing. She was at the courthouse the morning of the kidnapping. There's no way she took Gage, had time to drive him to Bel Air, and then arrive at the courthouse in time for court."

"Maybe someone else took him—the man in the video—and then handed him off to her later," Amber said.

"Why involve someone else?" Duke shook her head. "It increases her chances of someone talking. Look at the lengths she went to hide her identity in order to hire O'Neil and Kendell." Duke frowned. "Which brings up another thought. How did McGee know where and when to set up the stunt?"

"Because I pretty much drew her a map of our whole schedule, how we shared custody. Her questions about how we made it work seemed innocent enough at the time, but I can see now…she asked a *lot* of questions about routes we traveled and the logistics of it all. I thought it was weird, but I also thought she was just into me."

Amber groaned.

"She might have even been with me once when I picked up Gage from pre-school."

Amber crossed her arms and glared at him again. "Gage was in that house. I know it within the depths of my bones."

Duke sighed. "We can still do some digging. Tomorrow we'll talk to the neighbors and see if anyone saw the boy."

Amber frowned. "Why wait? Let's talk to the neighbors *now*."

Roy chuckled. "This is the ritzy side of town. Things don't work the same here."

His wife focused her raging glare on him once again. "What do you mean?"

Duke looked at her in the rearview mirror. "If we start knocking on doors in Bel Air at this hour, tomorrow morning the chief, councilman, the mayor, and maybe even the governor's phone would be ringing off the hook at eight tomorrow morning."

"And?"

He patted Amber's hand. "And the days of forging ahead with an investigation and inconveniencing influential witnesses are long gone. Nowadays, we have to schedule around their pickle ball games and visits to the plastic surgeon."

Duke smiled. "I can get enough info to verify McGee's nephew story tomorrow."

"She mentioned a housekeeper. You should talk to her as well." Roy placed a hand on the top of the front seat and inched forward. "Lavonne, is there any way we can get someone to sit on her house? If Gage *is* in there, we don't want her to move him."

"I've got the black-and-white sitting on the house until day watch. If anyone comes or goes tonight, they'll call me directly. I'll arrange for some plainclothes detectives to take their spot in the morning."

"She has my son all right," Amber said. "I just don't know what she did with him."

82

———

ROBYN

After the cops left, Robyn returned to Logan's room, and rechecked the closet, and all the nooks and crannies, and every place throughout the house she could think of that a little boy might hide. There was no sign of him.

Panic filled her. *Where in the hell is he?* She looked in her car and the garbage cans, then she grabbed a flashlight and checked the backyard. *What happened to my little boy?* Tears started to run down her cheeks, and then it hit her. *It can't be this easy, can it?* The police thought the boy was here…and he was. *I'm off the hook. They got nothing!* Her relief was replaced with dread. *Unless the police get a search warrant and come back. Fingerprints!* Logan's would be all over the house. *Wait! He's a little boy. He doesn't have fingerprints on file…right?*

She assured herself she didn't need to worry about that,

but a search warrant was something else. There was the stained shower curtain and hair color box in the garbage can. The clothes the boy had been wearing when she took him were at the bottom of the barrel as well. *I have to get rid of them! I should take care of that tonight, but what if the police have someone watching the house?*

Then she realized she had an even bigger problem—Rosa. *What if the cops talked to her?* Worse yet, she was sure the cops would want to verify her nephew story. Luckily, she had someone who owed her a favor.

83

AMBER

Once the detective sedan pulled into Devonshire Station and parked, the occupants exited slowly.

"Robyn McGee was the closest thing to a lead we've had, but I think we're done for tonight," Duke said, checking her watch. "I've barely slept in forty-eight hours.

Amber shook her head. "We need to press on."

Duke sighed and tilted her head. "And do what? I think we all need to rest. My partner and I will return to McGee's house tomorrow and try again to get a consent search. She probably won't agree, but then we'll at least push her for contact info for her sister and the housekeeper."

Amber shook her head. "Maybe it's time we bring in the FBI."

Duke stood taller. "That's *my* call, Officer Buckner. My decision, or the chief of police."

"I know that McGee woman knows where Gage is and you don't seem willing to do anything. Why don't you bring her in for questioning? Get her out of her comfort zone."

Roy nodded. "She's got a point, Lavonne. We could go back to the house, ask for the consent search. If she agrees, fine. We do the search and bring her in for questioning. Obviously, if she refuses the search, we'll have to come up with something else."

"I don't disagree with anything you've said. But we all need some rest." She looked at her watch again. "It's almost 0130 hours. Let's meet back here at 0600."

Duke and her partner went inside the station.

Roy looked at Amber. "She's right. We've got cops watching Robyn's house. We're all exhausted. Let's grab some sleep and start fresh in a couple of hours."

She glared at him. "Our boy is out there—"

"I know. But we're no good to him if we're too tired to think."

She crossed her arms and scowled. "Fine. I doubt I'll sleep, though. And tomorrow, if we're no closer to finding our son, I'm calling the chief personally and asking him to get the FBI involved."

84

DAZZLE

While Sugar kept things running at the Reseda house, Dazzle spent much of the evening scouting for a larger house to rent, one more secluded than the current house. This time, instead of poaching, he'd rent a place, so he'd spent his night on his phone in a coffee shop looking at house rentals. He wanted quality in a new property to operate his brothel and also needed new girls to add to his stable.

The Side Alley Cafe was right on one of the busiest prostitution tracks in the San Fernando Valley. Between jotting down addresses for potential rentals, he looked over the working girls as they took breaks from the chilly night air.

After narrowing his house search to three possibilities, he focused on the girls in the restaurant. It was easy to figure out which girls already worked for a pimp. They avoided his gaze and stayed only long enough to get warm. But the free-lancers were more leisurely and reluctant to go back to the windy and dark sidewalk.

At about 4:00, two girls came inside, plopped into a booth, and ordered breakfast.

Dazzle studied them while they ate. The taller, meatier of the two looked to be about seventeen. Her bleached blonde hair washed out her face, which was marred by meth sores.

That was the trouble with renegades—Nobody around to keep their drug habit under control.

The other girl looked to be about fifteen. Her hip bones were clearly visible underneath black leggings, and her upper body was downright skeletal. Her face was gaunt, and at one time, probably pretty, but now ruined by drug sores. They wouldn't last too long unless someone intervened.

They'll hate me at first, but they'll be better off in the long run. He sauntered over and slid in beside the smaller of the two girls. "Evening, ladies. How about you let me buy your breakfast?"

A wary look passed between them, but neither girl looked at him. If they did, in the hooker world, it signaled they were choosing him as their pimp.

The older one shifted her gaze firmly to the Formica tabletop. "Thanks. We appreciate the offer, but we work for ourselves."

The younger girl, amped and jittery, struggled to keep her gaze away from him.

He nudged her shoulder. "You must have to work hard to keep yourself straight."

She turned her head away and shrugged.

"Listen, I can protect you and get you off the street. I've got a house where you can each have your own bed. I treat my girls right. Think of it. No more long, cold nights on the track, waiting for dates. The clients book time to see *you*."

The girls kept their heads down, but looked at each other.

"I don't like to brag, but I'm the most generous daddy around. I charge more for my girls but then we split the money 60/40. You give a blow job for forty bucks; you get to keep twenty-four dollars." It was a lie, but they didn't know.

The older girl frowned. "Why would we do that? If we do a bj for thirty, we get to keep the whole thing."

He nodded. "Yes, you do, but you have to pay for a motel, all your food, getting your nails done, all the things needed to live a good life. I take care of all that." He looked at the younger one without an ounce of guilt at all his lies. "Looks like you've got a pretty good crack addiction. I can help. You girls aren't stupid. A lot of stuff on the street is laced with Fentanyl, and people are dying. I've got a trusted associate who provides drugs for my girls." Another lie.

The older girl started nibbling at a fingernail. "I don't know. I've stayed independent since I hit the street."

Reaching into his pocket, he brought out his phone and searched through the photos. "This is one of my girls." He pulled up the ad for Candi and turned the screen so they could both see. "Does she look like she's hurting?" He scrolled and found a great one of Sugar, Diamond, and Eden when they were all getting ready to go out and work in Vegas. The girls were excited that he had sprung for new outfits. "Here are my other girls. Tell me that they don't look fine. We were on vacation in Vegas." *Work, vacation…same difference.*

"You got any of that clean rocket fuel on you now?" the tiny one asked.

He shook his head. "I don't hold it, but I'll get you some. Let me pay for your breakfast, and I'll take you to meet my girls. If you don't like what you see, I'll bring you right back." He slapped a twenty on the table. "What are your names?"

The older one answered as they all slid out of the booth, "I'm Alyssa, and she's Jessica."

"Nice to meet you, ladies. I'm Dazzle McDaddy."

85

ROY

The next morning, Roy and Amber met Duke at Devonshire station.

Neither he nor Amber had slept much. They'd lain on her bed, back-to-back, until he'd heard her crying. He'd rolled over and held her, and they'd both fallen asleep.

As they walked out to the detective's car, Duke advised her partner wouldn't be joining them. "He has to be in court this morning on another case."

As Duke started the car, she got a text. She looked at her phone. "Robyn is on the move."

"Where is she heading?" Roy asked as he sat in the front passenger seat.

"East on Santa Monica Boulevard."

"Maybe going to the studios in Hollywood," Amber said from the backseat.

"Makes sense," said Duke. "I'll head that way."

"Hopefully, we can get inside to talk to her," Amber said.

Duke looked into the rearview mirror. "I worked Holly-wood Division as a sergeant. We usually had good coopera-tion from the studios."

"Let's get our priorities in order," Roy said. "What exactly do we want from her?"

"We want to talk to the housekeeper," Amber said.

Roy nodded. "We need contact info for the sister. I don't recall Robyn ever mentioning a sister…but then we weren't seeing each other very long."

Behind him, he heard Amber sigh.

Traffic was horrible on the Hollywood freeway. Roy was getting anxious and Amber's silent tension from the back seat filled the sedan.

He didn't think it was possible, but Amber's silent tension seemed to fill the car to overflowing as they exited the freeway at Gower. The sidewalks in the heart of Holly-wood were clogged with men and women, sleeping or passed out from alcohol or drugs.

"I doubt this is how most of America envisions the glamor of Hollywood," he murmured.

"Probably not," Duke said, pulling to the curb of a red zone behind a plain wrap detective car that had followed Robyn to the studio. "These detectives are from Devon-shire's gang unit. They replaced the black-and-white watching Robyn's house early this morning. I was lucky to get them…so be nice."

Two detectives exited their car, as did Roy, Amber, and Duke. The group rendezvoused on the sidewalk. After quick introductions, the gang cops relayed Robyn's activities, including her arrival at the studio twenty minutes earlier.

"We weren't sure if you wanted us to follow her inside or not."

Duke shook her head. "No. You did the right thing. We'll go try to talk to her. We're not sure she'll be willing to talk to us, so I'd like you to stay on her after we leave to see where she goes."

"Not a problem, Lavonne."

Duke looked at Amber, then at Roy. "Shall we?"

86

———

ROBYN

Robyn felt like crap with less than an hour of sleep after throwing Roy, his wife, and that detective out of her home. The walls were closing in, but there was hope.

The cops had shown up at her house thinking they'd catch her with Roy's son, but somehow the kid had disappeared. Although he'd vanished, it had been a blessing. She'd spent most of the night wiping every possible surface, including vacuuming the entire house, at least three times.

She'd debated whether or not it would look unnatural for her to wash Gage's bedding and make the bed, but fear of the police collecting DNA from the child's sheets had her washing everything in the middle of the night as well.

She pulled the garbage can just inside the garage, and with the aid of a broom, pulled the shower curtain, the discarded hair-dye products, and Gage's clothing out of the large bin and stuffed them into several plastic bags. She then placed the bags into a duffel before cramming it into the back of her Mercedes.

Although she'd passed through the wrought-iron gates at the studio hundreds of times, her heart throbbed as she waited for the uniformed security guard to check her studio pass and wave her through.

Her first stop was behind the art department, where the dumpsters were lined up against the high brick walls. She exited her vehicle and took the plastic bag holding the red-stained shower curtain along with Gage's underwear and socks to the trash receptacles and tossed it inside. She'd tied a knot at the top of the bag so the shower curtain wouldn't be visible if upended.

She threw the bag containing the hair dye packaging and implements into a second dumpster.

Next she drove over to the wardrobe department. The freshly washed clothes Gage had been wearing when she'd snatched him from his mother's car were secreted inside her large purse.

She entered the costuming area, with its rows and rows of colorful material and hangers stored behind a long counter almost the full width of the room. Men's clothing was on the left, ladies' wardrobe dominated the middle, and children's items were on the right.

The warehouse seemed deserted, so she headed to the children's racks organized by size and then color. The toddler-clothes in her purse would be near the front of the kid's racks.

Finding the right section, she searched for empty hangers. There wasn't a single one in sight.

She pulled the jeans and long-sleeved T-shirt out of her purse. Quickly draping his jeans over another pair already on the rack, she pulled his gray T-shirt onto a hanger covered by a black and gray flannel shirt.

She was returning the hangers to the rack just as a young woman with frizzy red hair bustled into the room.

"May I help you? You're not supposed to be in with the costumes."

"I was told that Chantal Wiggins was here looking for something to wear on her sitcom." Robyn lowered her voice, as if sharing a bit of gossip. "I hear she had a meltdown on the set and said if the costume designer couldn't find something decent for her to wear that she'd do it herself."

The young woman's eyes widened, and she glanced at the ladies' clothing. "I haven't seen her this morning," she said, walking toward the racks.

"Hmmm." Robyn trailed after her for a few feet. "Maybe my info was bad. I'll get out of your hair. Chantal has a wicked temper—especially so early in the morning. For your sake, I hope my source was wrong. Have a good day." Robyn waited until she was out of the wardrobe department to exhale. "That was close," she said to herself.

87

DAZZLE

Dazzle drove the girls from the restaurant to the house in Reseda. He could tell they were getting antsy, and maybe having second thoughts about going with him. "I'm taking you to the old house. We're moving to a bigger and better one later today. I'll get you settled in with my other girls."

Alyssa picked at a sore on her cheek. "How many other girls are there?"

"Four. Sugar, Diamond, Eden, and Kitty—although I don't have Kitty tricking yet. She has other duties." He saw a wary look pass between the two girls. "Look. You don't have to worry. My girls are happy with me."

He pulled into the driveway and motioned for the girls to get out and follow him.

They did.

The house was quiet.

"Everyone must still be asleep. We've been making a ton of money here." He poked his head down the hall. "Sugar! Get up and bring the other girls with you." He motioned toward the kitchen. "You want something to drink? I think we've got orange juice or some soda."

"Nah," said Jessica. "What I could use is a hit of the pipe. You said you'd get me some."

Damn whore. Talking to me like I owe her something. He held his temper in check and gave the tweaker a charming smile. "I'll have it for you in just a bit."

His four girls shuffled into the kitchen. In their sweats and T-shirts, they looked like refugees, not sex workers.

"Girls, I want you to meet Venus and Sapphire." If Alyssa and Jessica were upset at being renamed, they kept it to themselves. He pointed as he spoke. "That's Sugar, Eden, Kitty, and Diamond."

None of his girls looked thrilled at the newcomers.

His phone rang. "Get to know each other," he said, as he walked out of the room. "Yo, who's this?"

A stream of Spanish filled his ear, asking if it was true— he'd pay three thousand dollars for a child. The dude on the line had a little boy to sell.

Shit. I need all my money if I'm gonna get a bigger house. "Yes. Where is the boy?"

The caller continued in Spanish. "I have him. Where can I give him to you and get my money?"

In the background, Dazzle heard a crying child. "He isn't damaged or hurt, is he?"

"No, he's fine. Just scared."

Damn well better be. I can't sell the kid if he's damaged goods. Dazzle gave the guy directions for the exchange of the child. He hung up the phone and returned to the kitchen, zeroing in on Sugar. "I'm going to leave you in charge. I'm taking Kitty and Eden out for a bit." His gaze found Kitty's. "Go put on some blue jeans and a red top."

"I don't have a red top."

"Well, find one!" He looked at Eden. "You, too. Blue jeans and a T-shirt or something. You can't look like a 'ho." He gave her a double-take. "And do something with your hair."

Sugar pushed herself away from the counter. "Why does Eden get to go with you and Kitty. Can't I go?"

"Come here," he said, walking from the kitchen into the living room.

He'd chosen Eden for this task because of all his girls, she was the biggest, strongest, and meanest. If the contact tried to take the money and run, or anyone tried to accost them, he knew Eden would smack 'em down.

He waited until Sugar stood in front of him and kept his voice low. "I've got a business transaction to handle. I need you back here to keep the new girls in check, in case anything goes wrong while I'm out. You'll need to get things going for the move."

Her eyes widened and surprisingly filled with tears. "Where are you going?"

"To get a kid. I told you I was going to bring kids in. Today is the day."

Her facial features relaxed. "I was afraid you were going to turn Kitty out."

"Not yet. I need her to pick up the kid and take care of him. But her day is coming." He narrowed his eyes. "Why do you care? Any money she brings in makes us all better off, and the sooner we can get that house in the Hollywood Hills."

Sugar shrugged. "She's a pretty good kid...kind of innocent."

He scoffed. "Yeah, well, that innocence is going to bring in a ton of coin."

"What do you want me to do with those two new girls? They're nasty lookin'."

"I'm going to leave a rock for each of them. Let 'em smoke it. They need to take the edge off, and once they're high they'll be happy to help you move all our shit."

"The skinny one looks like she's been using too much."

"Yeah, I'll straighten her out, but I can't cut her off cold turkey. In the meantime, I want everyone to start packing up this place. Any furniture that's decent will go with us. Be sure to take that bar. It makes a great front desk. By the end of the day, we're going to have a new place to live...and work."

"Are you sure you aren't taking on more than you can handle?"

He slapped her hard across the face. "Don't you *ever* question me about what I can and what I can't handle, understand?"

She rubbed her face with her hand. "Yes, Daddy," she whispered, tears springing to her eyes.

"Good. Now, get moving. It's a busy day." He regretted hitting her, but she'd questioned him in front of the new girls, and then tried to tell him he was taking on too much.

Even his main girl needed to get tuned up every now and then to keep her in line. "I'm gonna take Diamond and rent a truck. She'll drive it back here so all you girls can start loading it up."

An hour and a half later, Dazzle sat in his SUV on the top floor of the parking structure at the local mall.

He'd already dropped Eden and Kitty off at a gas station across the street from the shopping center entrance with orders to walk through the mall, and out to the second level of the parking structure, and then take the elevator up to the top. There would only be a few empty cars parked on the upper deck at this time of day.

He slid down in his seat, with his pistol near his right thigh. From behind tinted windows, he watched as his girls arrived.

As instructed, they stood near the elevator. Kitty shaded her eyes from the bright sun, while Eden stood beside her with a brown paper bag tucked under her arm.

Kitty said something to Eden, and the pair moved a few steps away, where they could stand in the shade.

A couple of minutes later, a battered sedan drove into view.

The driver exited and reached into the car to pick up a little white boy with bright red hair. The kid looked three, maybe four.

The Hispanic approached the two girls.

As soon as the man set the boy down, Kitty, took the kid's hand…just as Dazzle had ordered her to do.

Eden handed over the paper bag to the man.

He looked inside the bag, returned to his car, and drove away.

Kitty and the little boy followed Eden as she returned to the elevator and stepped inside.

As soon as they were out of sight, Dazzle drove back to the gas station across the street…and waited.

88

———

ANTONIO

One quick text to Araceli—*Landing. Meet you out front*—and Antonio drummed his fingers on his knees as his flight from Reno to Burbank airport taxied to the gate. He'd slept most of the trip, so he was energized and ready to go back to the brothel and, hopefully, rescue Brooke.

Ten minutes later, he was in his sister's car. "Hey, drive me through that McDonalds. I'm hungry. I'll buy you an early lunch."

She did as he asked, and as they pulled away from the burger joint, she glanced at him. "What's your game plan for getting Brooke?"

"I want to talk to Payton before we do anything. I need to know if she's ever seen Dazzle with a gun, if he has any other muscle around, and anything she can tell me about the layout of the house."

"I don't think she's going to be able to help you there. He beat her after they'd rolled a trick. It was her first night, and she was in the hospital after that. I don't think she ever got to the Reseda house."

"Well, I'll talk to her, then go over to the brothel."

Within half an hour, he and Araceli were at Victims of the Street sitting with the young girl he'd known as Candi.

"Do you remember me?"

"You were my savior date."

He smiled. "My name is Antonio, and I'm Araceli's brother. I want to help you get Brooke away from your pimp so we can get you and your sister home."

The girl's eyes filled with tears. "I can't believe I was so stupid. He's probably got Brooke working the streets by now." Her tears started to fall.

"Payton, listen to me. We're going to get her back safely. Before we can do that, though, I need to know all about your pimp and his operation."

After hearing how they'd met and everything that had happened since Dazzle McDaddy had picked Payton and her sister up in Utah, Antonio felt he had enough info to go looking for Brooke. "Thank you, Payton. My sister and I are going to find her."

"I want to go, too," Payton said.

"I'm sure you do," Araceli said. "But we can't risk it."

Antonio nodded. "It could tip off McDaddy that we're onto him."

The girl scowled.

"I promise we'll call you as soon as we know something solid."

Araceli smiled. "You can hang out here, and I'll call Linda the moment I know anything. I promise. I haven't lied to you yet."

"Okay," the girl said, softly. "Tell Brooke I love her and I'm so sorry."

Antonio rose from the couch. "Once we find her, you can tell her yourself."

Later, they turned the corner onto the street where Dazzle's operation was housed, and Antonio pulled to the curb. "Celi, why don't you get out here? I'll pull up in front of the house. Just walk down the street in case something goes sideways. If it does, call 911."

"Good idea. Nobody visits a whorehouse with a girl sitting in their car outside." She opened the door and stepped out.

"Got your phone?"

She held it up. "Be careful."

"You, too." He eased toward the front of the house he'd visited the day before. "What the…" He frowned and threw the car into park, waiting until Celi came up to the passenger side of the car and got in.

"What's wrong?" She glanced at the house.

"The place looks different—abandoned, like no one is here. That doesn't make any sense." He turned the car off and stepped out. "Stay here but slide down in case someone *is* in there." Slamming the door behind him, he jogged across the lawn toward the front porch.

As expected, no one responded to his knock.

He cupped his hands at his temples and peered into the

large porch window. He could see the area where he'd sat the night before, but there was no counter, no couch…no other furniture in sight.

He tried the doorknob, but the door was locked.

Antonio turned toward the street and motioned to his sister that he was going to go around the back.

Celi nodded and gave him a thumbs up.

He went around to the side of the house and through a chain-link gate that led to the rear.

The glass in the rear door was broken, so he reached through the open pane and unlocked the door.

He strode through the house, noticing a number of fast-food wrappers and containers strewn on the counters and floors. Rooms that had served as the massage rooms were empty.

They'd packed up and gone.

He retraced his steps.

In the front yard of the house across the street, his sister was talking to an older man.

Antonio joined them.

"Antonio, this is Mr. Benson. I was asking him when the people in the house across the street moved out."

The old man bobbed his head at him. "I knew the minute they showed up they were up to no good. A flashy thug and a passel of young girls."

Antonio nodded. "When did they leave?"

"This morning. Not long ago at all. They packed up all their crap—" he glanced at Araceli, "Pardon my language, Miss. They hauled all their stuff into a bob-tail truck and took off." He frowned and shook his head. "Those girls moved furniture, some kind of heavy bar or something, and what little junk they brought with them."

"How long had they lived there?" Araceli asked.

"That's the crazy thing. They only moved in the day before yesterday. What was that, Monday?" He grinned and nodded. "Yeah, Monday."

Antonio smiled. "I don't suppose you got the license plate of that bob-tail truck, did you?"

The old man waved his hand, like brushing a fly away. "Nah, I was glad to see them go. I knew exactly what was goin' on over there. They brought all kinds of riffraff into the neighborhood. Just terrible."

Antonio held out his hand. "Well, thank you very much for your help."

The man shook his hand, and he and Araceli started back to their car.

"Hey, young man!" Mr. Benson motioned for him to return.

Surprised, Antonio walked back toward the man.

The old man's rheumy eyes bore into his. "You got a nice girl there. You need to treat her with respect. I may be old, and I may not hear so good, but my eyes work perfectly fine. I didn't want to say anything in front of your lady-friend, but I'm certain I saw your car parked in front of that cat house yesterday afternoon. You need to shape up or you're gonna lose your girlfriend."

89

———

AMBER

Amber sat in the rear seat of Duke's detective ride as they pulled up to the guard stationed at the entrance to the studios.

"Good morning, may I help you?"

Duke smiled and showed her ID card. "I'm Detective Duke from the LAPD. I need to talk to one of the casting directors who is on the premises."

Concern crossed the man's face. "Is everything all right?"

"Yes, everything is fine. We just need to speak to Robyn McGee. I believe she checked in about forty-five minutes ago."

"I remember." The guard nodded. "Ms. McGee did come through a while ago."

"Where would we find her?"

He looked puzzled. "I'm not sure. We don't document where pass-holders are going."

On the opposite side of the guard shack, a car drove through the exit of the studio gates.

"Oh, there she is now." He cupped his hands around his mouth. "Miss McGee!"

The Mercedes SUV turned right and continued down the street.

Duke threw the car in reverse, backed out of the driveway, and sped after McGee. "Hit the red light," she said to Roy.

He flipped the apparatus down so the red light glowed forward through the windshield.

The narco detectives were right behind them.

The Mercedes continued until the driver stopped at a stop sign.

Duke flipped a switch, allowing her to use the siren by pressing on the horn. She gave a short blast and motioned for McGee to pull over.

McGee glanced in her rearview mirror and sped up.

"Aw, jeez…she's running," Roy muttered.

After about a hundred yards, the SUV abruptly pulled to the curb.

Roy and Amber were the first out of the car, and Roy crossed over to the driver's side. Amber acted as the cover officer and approached the passenger side.

Robyn rolled down her window.

"Turn off the engine," Roy ordered.

"This is ridiculous. Why do you people keep harassing me?"

"Turn off the car."

Robyn did so and opened the driver's door.

Roy grabbed her arm and pulled her to the sidewalk where Duke and Amber waited.

Amber noticed the narco detectives had pulled to the curb, several vehicle lengths away, and watched from their car.

Robyn crossed her arms, and her lips formed a thin line, as she rocked from, side-to-side. "What is it with you? Now you're following me to work?"

Duke stepped forward. "We just needed some additional information."

"Well, why didn't you call me?"

"We didn't have your number. You threw us out, remember?"

Robyn looked at Roy. "You deleted me from your phone?" She scoffed and shook her head. "What do you want?"

Amber pulled a notepad out of her pocket. "We need the contact information for your housekeeper and your sister."

The redhead sighed. "My phone is in my purse."

Roy moved toward the passenger door. "I'll get it."

"Why? You worried I've got a gun in my car?"

He retrieved the purse and, before handing it to her, glanced inside through the unzipped top.

Amber wondered if Robyn realized he *was* checking for weapons.

He handed the casting director her purse.

She pulled out her phone and began tapping the screen before looking at Amber. "Ready?"

Amber nodded.

"Rosa Juarez." She then rattled off a phone number.

"Do you have an address for her?"

Robyn sighed and then recited an address in the Valley.

"And your sister?" Amber transferred the woman's Palmdale contact information in her notebook as Robyn spoke.

"She may not get back to you right away. She's a busy woman," Robyn warned.

"Don't worry," Duke said. "We'll talk to her."

"I hope you don't harass her like you are me." Robyn looked at the detective. "Am I free to go now? I've got things to do."

Amber held up her notepad. "Why don't you give me your cell number, so if we have further questions, we can call—and you won't feel so harassed."

90

BROOKE

Brooke's heart pounded and her hands trembled as she and Eden walked through the mall with the little boy. She considered breaking away from Eden with the little boy and running into a store, begging for help. She didn't know what was going on, but whatever they were doing, it wasn't right. Why else would Dazzle have them acting like spies?

"Don't get any big ideas about running off with the kid," Eden sneered. "I'm faster than you. Daddy gave me a job to do, and I'm not going to take a beating because I let you get away."

The little boy stopped. "Pee pee."

Brooke bent over and asked quietly, "You have to go potty?"

He nodded.

Eden looked down at the boy. "Too bad. Hold it."

Brooke straightened. "Eden, he's little. He can't do that. Look," she said, pointing. "There are bathrooms down there."

Eden resumed walking toward the exit.

"Daddy won't like it if he pees in the car," Brooke said. "It will only take a minute."

Eden scowled. "All right. But make it fast."

Brooke hoped Eden would wait outside, and she could ask someone in the bathroom for help. It was a wasted wish.

Not only was the bathroom empty, but Eden used the facilities while Brooke helped the boy.

Ten minutes later, the trio approached Dazzle as he paced outside his car.

When he caught sight of them, he shook his head and climbed behind the wheel.

Eden got into the passenger seat, while Brooke and the boy got into the back.

"Where in the hell have you been?"

"The kid had to piss," Eden replied.

Dazzle twisted around in his seat and grinned at the boy. "Hello, little man. I'm your new daddy."

Brooke saw a look of confusion on the boy's face.

Dazzle started the car. "Okay, let's get this show on the road. I'm taking you girls to our new house." He glanced at Eden. "I've got to sign some papers, pay the guy, and pick up the keys. We're going to pretend to be a married couple with our two kids."

Eden's eyebrow shot up. "You think he'll believe I'm old enough to have a kid Kitty's age?"

"Good point. Then there's the whole skin thing. I'm

black, and you're Latino. How in the hell did we have two white kids, especially one with red hair?" He looked in the rearview mirror at Brooke. "You and the boy will stay in the car. No one can know you're in here. Understand?"

She nodded.

They drove into a neighborhood at the base of the foothills and pulled into the driveway of a large two-story house with a sporty BMW parked at the curb.

Eden got out as Dazzle twisted in his seat to face her.

"Keep him quiet. Don't even think about running away. If you do, I'll kill your sister, and then I'll go back to Boise and kill your parents." He smiled. "Remember, I know where they live." He exited the car and slammed the door.

Brooke watched as Dazzle put his arm around Eden, even kissing her ear, as they made their way to the front door.

Before they could knock, the door was opened, and they were ushered inside.

Brooke turned to the boy next to her. "What's your name?"

His chin began to wobble and tears filled his eyes. "Mama."

She gave him a hug. "I know. I want my mother, too." She took his hand in hers. "I'm going to figure out a way that we both get to see our mommies." She smiled at him. "My name is Brooke. Can you say that?"

"Book."

She grinned and repeated it, emphasizing the *R* in her name.

"Book," he said and giggled.

"Close enough. What's your name?"

"Cage."

She tilted her head at him. "Cage?"

He nodded.

What a strange name. A vibrating noise from the center console caught her attention. Dazzle's phone sat against the dashboard charging. *I can call for help!*

The phone's screen lit up again, displaying a text message.

Brooke surged between the front seats and read the text.

10 large for the package. You having any trouble with it? The screen darkened again.

Plopping back into her seat, she knew the package mentioned must be Cage. *Get help!*

Pushing forward again, and with shaking hands, she picked up Dazzle's phone.

PART X

91

———————

ROSA

Rosa had been upset since yesterday, when Miss Robyn had screamed at her about taking care of Logan. Her employer's last words to her had been that she expected to see her on Thursday.

Rosa still wasn't sure she wanted to go back to the mansion in Bel Air. She worked hard to build a good reputation and was beloved by all her employers—until now. Some of her clients blew up at any number of situations in their lives, but no one had ever directed their anger at her. Even the ones who were drunk or high during their Hollywood meltdowns seemed to keep themselves in check around the help, especially Rosa.

Wednesdays were her only real day off and she sat on her couch lingering over her coffee while watching an episode of Dr. Phil she'd recorded earlier in the week.

Her cell phone rang, and she glanced at the screen but didn't recognize the number. *If it's important, they'll leave a message.*

She no sooner had that thought, and her phone chimed.

She paused Dr. Phil and retrieved the message.

Good morning. This call is for Rosa Juarez. This is Officer Amber Buckner from the Los Angeles Police Department. I'd like to meet with you. You may have information about an incident we're investigating. It should only take a few minutes. The officer left a phone number.

She didn't have information about any incident. *What could they want?* With trembling fingers, she returned the call.

"Buckner."

"This is Rosa Juarez. You just left me a message."

"Thank you for returning my call. Ms. Juarez, I'm working on a missing child report. You may have some information about the case. May I come speak with you?"

"I don't know anything about a missing boy." Rosa immediately thought of Logan McGee, and in an instant, the box of red hair dye in the trash can made sense.

"Please. We need your help. I can come to you, and I promise, I won't take a lot of your time."

Rosa sighed and recited her address.

"Thank you. I should be there in less than an hour."

True to her word, the officer rang Rosa's doorbell about forty-five minutes later.

Rosa peeked out the door. A nice-looking woman held up an LAPD badge. "Don't you have a partner?"

The woman looked surprised. "I was sent to see if you have any information concerning our case. If you don't, we haven't wasted the time of two officers. If you do, we'll contact you later for a formal statement."

It made sense to Rosa, so she ushered the officer into her small bungalow home in North Hollywood.

The officer had a pleasant smile. In her black jeans, gray sweater, and neutral-painted fingernails, she looked nothing like Rosa imagined a police officer would look.

"Thank you for meeting with me."

Rosa motioned for the woman to take a seat. "Would you like some coffee? It's fresh."

"Thank you, I'm good," she said, taking a seat on the sofa.

"What is this all about, officer?"

"Please, call me Amber. It's my understanding, you work for a woman named Robyn McGee. Is that correct?"

Rosa nodded. "For about five years—every Thursday."

"Have you ever met Robyn's sister?"

"Her sister? No." Rosa hesitated. "I didn't know she had one."

"So, you've never met the sister or her little boy?"

"I'm sorry, no."

"Did you ever ask Robyn about the bedroom set up like a train?"

"That room is for Logan."

The officer tensed. "Who's Logan?"

"The little boy Miss Robyn adopted."

Amber pulled her phone from the back pocket of her jeans and pulled up a photo and turned the screen for Rosa to see. "Is this Logan?"

Rosa looked at the photo. There was no doubt it was a

photo of Logan—and nodded. "He has red hair now. I think Miss Robyn dyed it."

The officer's eyes watered, as though she might cry. "This boy was kidnapped two days ago, on Monday morning. Do you know where he is now?"

Rosa shook her head. "I would assume with Miss Robyn."

Amber explained that they'd gone to Robyn's home the night before. The boy hadn't been there, but the bed was unmade. "Do you have any idea where he might be, or where she might hide him?"

Rosa shook her head. "No, and I can't believe that Miss Robyn would steal a child."

"I need you to tell me everything that Robyn said about the boy and adopting him."

I went to work at Miss Robyn's house last Thursday, as usual. That day was the first I heard about her adopting a boy. I helped her prepare the bedroom for the boy's arrival in a couple of days.

"But the bedroom…didn't you think it was odd she had a train-themed bedroom?"

"The train room was built between my previous visit and my workday last Thursday. She said the prop department had made it for her."

"You said Ga—the boy has red hair now."

Rosa nodded. "I saw a box of hair dye in the garbage can. There was also a shower curtain that was stained with the dye."

"Did Robyn say anything about taking the boy someplace? Does she have any close friends who might watch him?"

"She doesn't know much about children and had difficulties getting the boy to do exactly what she wanted, so she asked that I come help on Tuesday, but she never mentioned anything about taking him anywhere," Rosa said.

"Do you think she'd hurt the boy?"

"I don't know. She slapped him when he wouldn't lie down for a nap."

"Is there anyone else who might know about the boy or showed interest in him?"

"I'm sorry. Miss Robyn is usually very busy with her work." Rosa rubbed her hands together while she thought. "Wait. There was a man. It's been some time ago, but she liked him a lot. Rob, Ron…I'm sorry. I don't remember his name."

"Roy?"

"Yes! Roy, something or other." Rosa smiled. "He was a police officer, too. She might have told him. She said he was a good family man, and if things worked out, she hoped they'd have a family together." The housekeeper leaned closer and dropped her voice to a conspiratorial whisper. "He had just split with his wife, and I think Miss Robyn hoped he would marry her."

92

ROY

Roy and Lavonne Duke sped along the 14 Freeway on their way to meet with Robyn's sister, Kirsten Vaughn, and her little boy in Palmdale.

With Duke's partner still in court, she'd decided to split their interviews with the housekeeper and the sister separately.

Duke had decided that Amber would check out Rosa Juarez, while she and Roy made the hour drive north of Los Angeles to the sister's house. If it looked as if Rosa had valuable info, Duke would have someone other than Amber re-interview the housekeeper.

"What's our next move if Robyn's sister's story checks out about her son staying in Bel Air with Robyn?" Roy asked, steering the sedan smoothly through traffic.

Duke shrugged. "If that happens, we're going to have to

start over. With you and Robyn having a prior relationship, I don't think it's a coincidence she's on our radar."

They exited the Antelope Valley Freeway and drove east.

Pulling to the curb a few doors down from their target, they took in the older, decayed subdivision of bungalow-style houses. The Vaughn house was in desperate need of paint.

He scanned the front yard. "I don't see any toys or bikes or anything to indicate a kid lives here."

Duke chuckled. "This isn't a neighborhood where you'd leave anything of value in the yard. It would be gone in seconds." She opened the passenger door. "Let's see what Robyn's sister has to say."

An attractive brunette opened the door and smiled. "Please, come in," she said, gesturing toward a tiny living room. Unlike the outside, the interior of the home screamed that at least one child lived here. Raw lumber shelves rested on cement cinder blocks, with scores of mini cars, and trains filling the surfaces. Kirsten offered them a place to sit, but they declined.

"We're in a bit of a time crunch. We just need to verify with you that your son stayed with your sister last weekend…and we'd like to ask him a few questions."

The woman frowned. "I'd like to help you out, but Joey is with his father this week." Her face brightened. "But we did stay with my sister Robyn last weekend. We had a great time. We went to Universal Studios."

"Sounds like fun," Roy said. "I bet Joey really likes his firehouse bedroom. That gigantic fire-engine bed is really cool."

Kirsten nodded. "I have a terrible time getting him to

come home." She motioned toward the living room. "Going to my sister's house is like going to a palace compared to living here."

Duke smiled. "How often do you and Robyn get to visit?"

Wariness filled the woman's eyes. "It kind of depends on Robyn's schedule. She's very busy."

Roy pulled out an FI from his pocket, took down Kirsten's full name and address, as well as the name and address of her boy's father. "What about your employer? What do you do for a living?"

"Have you seen the commercial for the Night Sun Motion Activated Security Lights? I'm the woman that gets mugged walking to her front door." She beamed.

Roy jotted more notes on the card in his hand while Duke nodded.

"I'm afraid you're going to have to come with us." He returned the FI and pen to his pocket. "You're lying."

Outrage filled Kirsten's face. "You're wrong. That *is* me getting mugged. I can prove it. You just don't recognize me. They had me wear a blonde wig. I have the raw video on my computer."

Duke sighed. "We believe you about the commercial, but you are *not* Robyn McGee's sister."

Kirsten stood up straighter. "How dare you! I'm trying to help you, and you insult me? I think you'd better leave."

Roy shrugged. "Have it your way. Turn around and put your hands behind your back—palms together."

"Wha-no! I'm not going to do that."

Duke leaned in toward the woman. "Let's cut the B.S.,

Kirsten. Robyn McGee's house doesn't have a fire truck bed, but it does have a bed in the form of a train."

Kristen's face paled.

"Now, you can tell us what you know, or we can arrest you for obstructing an investigation—and that will probably turn into conspiracy, and then into kidnapping. So, you tell me…what's it gonna be?"

93

BROOKE

rooke glanced at the house. There was no sign of
Dazzle or Eden, so with trembling hands, she
pushed the button on Dazzle's phone.

The little boy watched with wide eyes.

"Oh, no," she murmured. "I need his fingerprint." *Now
what, Brooke?* "Cage, I don't know what to do. I'm scared."

The boy looked up at her. "Mama."

Run! Her heart pounded and her eyes burned with fresh
tears. *You can't run. Dazzle will kill Payton…and Mom and Dad,
too.* She had to save this boy, though. She didn't know what
Dazzle had planned for either of them, but she knew it
wasn't good. *Payton may already be dead.*

Sugar's words rang in her ears. *'If Dazzle didn't bring
Candi home, your sister isn't coming…ever.'*

This might be our only chance. She took a deep breath and

slowly blew it out. "Okay, Cage, listen to me. I need you to run very fast and be very quiet. Can you do that? We have to get away from the bad man."

The boy, nodded.

She took another deep breath. "Okay, let's go." Glancing at the house one more time, she saw Eden looking out a second-floor window at the SUV. Brooke waved, then waited until the curtains fell back into place. "Okay, Cage, now." Slowly, she opened the SUV door farthest away from the house.

Jumping down, she turned and extended her arms.

Cage let her lift him down.

She pushed the rear door carefully. It looked closed, but wasn't latched. She couldn't risk making any noise to alert Dazzle. The interior light stayed on, but she didn't think it would be visible in the sunlight.

She grabbed the boy's hand. "Run Cage," she whispered and began jogging down the sidewalk. *Now what? Do I try one of these houses? What if a murderer lives there? Pick a nice house… one that has kids toys or something. Maybe a nice woman will answer.*

It didn't take the little boy long to run out of energy. "I tired." He extended his arms. "Up."

Knowing time wasn't on their side, she scooped him into her arms. He weighed a ton. She knew she wouldn't make it far carrying him, but she needed to get off this block.

Two houses from the corner, she saw a house with a basketball hoop out front. "Come on Cage. Let's try this one." She slowed to a walk, set the boy back on his feet, and took his hand.

Walking to the front door, she tried to think of the best thing to say to anyone who answered.

She rang the bell, then leaned her head toward the door listening for movement.

Not hearing anything, she pressed the doorbell again.

Oh, no! "No one's here, Cage. Come on." She grabbed the boy's hand, but before they left the porch, she peeked her head around the stucco corner and looked down the street.

Dazzle's SUV stood, undisturbed in the driveway of the rental house.

"Let's go. We'll look for help on the next block."

94

———

AMBER

As Amber walked back to her car from Rosa's house, she called Roy.

"Buckner," he answered.

"Roy, I'm just leaving Rosa Juarez's house. You'll be happy to know that Robyn McGee thought you were a good family man, and she hoped to have a family with you." Her jovial words dripped with sarcasm, but she didn't care. Everything pointed to Robyn McGee kidnapping their child —and it was Roy's fault for getting involved with the woman.

"You can calm down. We just spoke to Robyn's *supposed* sister. The whole thing was a lie. We're going to arrest Robyn."

"For kidnapping?"

"We're going to start with obstruction, but I'm sure once

we get more evidence, we'll be increasing the charges."

"Great, but we still don't know where Gage is."

"I know," he snapped. "I'm sorry. Yelling at you isn't going to tell us what she did with Gage."

"Obviously, she sold him. Maybe she needed money to maintain that big house in Bel Air." Amber told him what Rosa had said about the hair dye and shower curtain in the trash barrel. "We'll want to include that in the warrant."

"We'll also send SID to Robyn's house for prints and DNA collection."

"What do you need me to do?"

Roy hesitated. "Can you call Antonio? He called while we were interviewing the 'sister.' He said he had some important information."

"Yeah, I'll give him a call. What else?"

"Why don't you meet us at Dev station? You can go with us when we arrest Robyn."

"Okay. I'll see you there." At a red light she dialed Antonio's number. "Antonio, it's Amber. Roy said you'd called. We're about to make an arrest in Gage's kidnapping, so he can't call you back. What's up?"

"You found Gage?" Jubilation filled his voice. "That's great! Is he okay?"

"We don't have Gage, but we have a pretty good idea who took him. The only problem is that we think she may have sold him." She paused. "I don't want to be rude, but what did you want?"

"First off, I found Candi, the young hooker I've been looking for. Her real name is Payton—"

"Wait! Was she in the hospital after being beat up by her pimp?"

"Yeah, she definitely took a beating from her pimp. How did you know?"

"Because she and her pimp jacked a trick early Sunday morning. Roy and I went and tried to get information from her at the hospital. How did you find her?"

"The hospital called Victims of the Street, and Araceli picked her up and brought Payton to the shelter."

"Has she been talking to you? She wouldn't even tell me her name."

"That's because her pimp has her eleven-year-old sister, Brooke."

"That explains why she wouldn't talk. Eleven is pretty young. Did she say anything about her pimp working younger kids?"

"No, but Araceli and I are trying to track the pimp to get Brooke back."

"Do you have any leads?"

"Looks like the pimp, Dazzle, took his girls off the street and has started doing in-call service."

"How many girls does he have?"

"Not counting Brooke, three. I found the house the pimp was using, and yesterday, I talked with a working girl named Sugar. I asked if she'd heard anything about someone dealing in kids. She said no, but her face said otherwise." He sighed. "Unfortunately, Araceli and I just went over to the house again, but they're gone. The neighbor said we just missed them."

"Did you learn anything else about Sugar or her pimp?"

"No, but she had two tats—a crown on her left wrist and a dollar sign on the back of her neck." He gave her a brief physical description of Sugar.

Amber turned into the parking lot of Devonshire station and parked. "That's not much to go on, but I can give it a shot. I'll check with vice and search the databases."

"She said the pimp's name is Dazzle McDaddy."

"That might help, although those guys change street names like we change our underwear. Thanks, and if I find anything out, I'll get back to you." She ended the call, hurried into the station, and went upstairs to the Vice Unit.

The office door was locked, and Amber checked the time. It was too early in the day for the officers to be working, as most vice crime occurred after dark.

She entered the detective squad room, and a detective walked toward her. "I'm working with Detective Duke. Is there an available computer I can use?"

He directed her to a nearby cubicle. "Torres called in sick today. You might want to wipe down the keyboard and desk before you get to work."

Amber nodded and grabbed an antiseptic wipe and cleaned the surfaces before logging on to the department website and related databases. Her expectations weren't great with what little she had to go on—Sugar; a common name for prostitutes, branded with two tattoos common to prostitutes, and a pimp named Dazzle.

She searched the Field Interview database, and even with the tattoo info included, there were just too many whores going by the name Sugar.

She focused on the pimp. She entered the nickname Dazzle and narrowed her search to the known prostitution tracks in the Valley.

One result was a guy who'd been questioned at a known motel used by prostitutes. Police were sent to a radio call of a domestic disturbance. When the officers arrived, there was a guy leaving the room where the disturbance was reported. He must have gone to his car because there was a black SUV listed on the FI card. The potential suspect, whose driver's license ID'd him as Monroe Peck, said his nickname was Daz.

Using Peck's FI card information, she found the officers had also interviewed a female who ID'd herself as Eden Smith.

But what really caught Amber's attention, Eden had identified Peck as Dazzle McDaddy. *Only a pimp would give themselves such an idiotic name.* However, his stupidity led her to Dazzle McDaddy's SeeMe social media page, and…jackpot!

The last entry were photos of a large house with the caption: *Lookin' like this will be the new digs for me and my girls.*

She checked the time stamp. It was from the night before.

Amber's fingers flew over the keyboard as she copied the photo's identifying information and put it into a photo search app.

Seconds later, she was on a real-estate website, where the house was listed for rent…along with its address. "Shadow Hills right off the 210, near Sunland," she whispered, jotting down the address.

Before she left Dazzle's SeeMe page, she scrolled through the previous weeks' worth of photos, hoping to see a picture of Gage. Instead, there were the usual—piles of money, fat cigars, and girls' boobs and asses.

She logged off the computer, jumped out of the chair, and ran to her car.

95

ROBYN

Robyn drove home from the studio, constantly checking her rearview mirror. "Relax," she said. "You've disposed of any sign that the Buckner boy was ever in your house." She still wondered what had happened to the kid.

Had he gotten out of her house? Had someone come in and taken him? That was impossible. She had a burglar alarm—but the alarm was only good if it had been turned on. When she'd had a few cocktails, she sometimes forgot to activate the security device.

The idea of a stranger coming into her house while she was sleeping was terrifying.

Who would have the nerve? She giggled as she considered the possibility that she was being pranked. *That's it! If I ever get questioned, I'll just say Roy, or even Amber, took him. They're framing me.* A wave of relief washed over her, as the cloud of worry that had filled her last twelve hours lifted.

Just the same, she decided to go through the house again wiping down any surfaces that Roy's son might have touched.

Even with her new alibi, there was still the probability of someone coming into her home and snatching the boy. *But who would do that?* Only one name came to mind. *Rosa.*

The housekeeper hadn't felt Robyn was capable of taking care of the boy, and she had a key to the house. Gage had met Rosa and liked her, so he wouldn't have cried when the maid came and pulled him out of bed.

As Robyn drove through the ornate gates of Bel Air, jealousy and anger filled her. She gripped the steering wheel with white knuckles. "How *dare* she come into my home and take my adopted son." And then she grinned. It was another alibi dropping into her lap.

"You can say that Rosa and Roy colluded to frame you." Her grin turned into an outright laugh. "You're untouchable, girl. You keep thinking, and you'll have a whole cast of people who might have snatched the kid."

96

DAZZLE

Dazzle shook hands with the property manager. With the contract signed, he was antsy to get back out to the car and check on the two kids.

Unfortunately, the property manager was a chatty guy and was still trying to *sell* Dazzle on the house. "This is the perfect street to live on. You've got the canyon in front of you, the hills behind you, with the freeway behind them." His tone took on a serious note. "The freeway is an excellent fire break."

"Yes, I'm sure we'll be very happy," Dazzle said, taking Eden's elbow and leading her toward the front door.

"Here are your keys," the guy said, dangling a keyring.

Dazzle took the keys. "Thank you. We'd better get a move on. We'll be moving in later today." As soon as he approached his car, he knew something was wrong. The interior light was on in his SUV and there was no sign of either kid. "Come on Eden. We need to hustle."

Beside him, the girl tensed. "Yeah." She turned to the property manager. "Thank you. It was nice to meet you."

They jogged to the car and got inside.

With the property manager watching, Dazzle willed himself to not explode with the anger coursing through his body. He plastered a fake grin on his face and waved at the guy climbing into his BMW. "I can't believe that little bitch would run."

Eden nodded. "I looked out the window of the house just a few minutes ago and Kitty waved to me."

"Then they can't be far. Keep your eyes peeled."

As soon as the property manager was out of sight, Dazzle swung the SUV out of the driveway, and down the street. His thinking was that the kids wouldn't run uphill. "Fuck!" He slammed his hands on the steering wheel. "Look on porches, behind trees, anywhere they might hide. That boy is worth ten grand."

They came to a side street, and he turned. "I'm going to kill that bitch, Kitty. I should'a broke her in along with her sister in Vegas."

Eden kept her gaze glued outside the window. "If I get to them first, Daddy, I'll make her pay. You know I will."

97

ROY

"I feel like we've spent our entire day driving on LA freeways," Roy complained, as they headed to Devonshire Station from Kirsten Vaughn's house.

"At least we didn't have to arrest Vaughn," Duke said. "Her statement about Robyn asking her to lie about being sisters and Kirsten's son staying at Robyn's over the weekend pretty much seals the deal."

"I don't give a shit about that. I just want to know where my son is."

Duke nodded. She was texting on her phone. "The detectives followed Robyn home from the studio. They're parked down the street from her house."

"Great." His cell phone rang. He didn't even look at the screen before answering. "Buckner."

"Roy, it's me. I've ID'd the pimp. His name is Monroe

Peck. He goes by the alias Dazzle McDaddy. I know where he's moving. In fact, I'm heading there now."

"Does he have Gage?"

"I don't know. I searched his social media and didn't see any photos of kids."

"You've got a patrol unit and a supervisor going with you, right?"

"I thought I'd check it out first. He may not even be there."

"No. Get some uniformed officers and notify the watch commander."

"Roy, if he sees black-and-whites in the neighborhood, he'll rabbit. If I can get into position, I can direct plain clothes units in and we can set a perimeter and get him."

"Amber, you're a P-2. You need supervision, more units and an air unit. Where's the house?"

"On Hillview Terrace, in Shadow Hills. I'm almost there. I'll call you back when I know more."

"Amb—"

The line disconnected.

"Damn her!"

He quickly relayed the conversation to Duke.

"Start heading that way. I'll call Foothill and get them rolling, along with an airship." Duke punched at her cell phone screen. "Lieutenant Murphy, this Lavonne Duke from Dev. I'm in charge of the Gage Buckner kidnapping." She quickly relayed all relevant information. "The guy we're looking for is Monroe Peck, aka Dazzle McDaddy. Amber Buckner is off duty and on her way to some house McDaddy is allegedly renting on Hillview Terrace in Shadow Hills. She's by herself." Duke listened for a second.

"*I* didn't tell her to go there. She's one of yours at Foothill. Maybe if *you* call her, she'll stop acting like Jane Wayne and listen to reason."

Roy gave Duke the description and license plate number of Amber's car.

"Ask them to get an air unit to look for her." Duke ended the call. "The WC didn't sound too happy. We don't have much info, but he'll get their detectives searching the databases for Peck. If Amber found McDaddy's information, they can too."

Roy's body hummed with irritation. Picking up Robyn McGee was a waste of time with this new lead. He knew Robyn didn't have his son. "We need to go to Foothill. I think Amber might be close to finding Gage."

"I agree. I'll have the narco guys who are sitting on Robyn's house take her into custody. Let's see if we can find Amber before she gets herself into trouble."

98

BROOKE

rooke's heart pounded from her chest all the way through her ears. After she and Cage dashed around the corner and onto the next block, none of the first few houses looked as though children lived in them.

Brooke led Cage along the front of the houses, but stayed off the sidewalk. She knew as soon as Dazzle realized they'd run away, he'd come after them. They'd be easy to spot on the sidewalk.

The sound of squealing tires turning onto the street had her pulling Cage behind some bushes.

She covered the boy with her body, ignoring the branches scratching her face. She couldn't see, but heard the car zoom past.

Looking through the shrub's limbs, she saw it was

Dazzle's black SUV pulling away. "He passed us, Cage. He passed us." She stood and pulled the boy to his feet. "Come on. We've got to find someone who can help us." She looked toward the front door of the closest house. "Let's try this one. Whoever answers can't be any scarier than Dazzle."

They jogged to the front porch, and she pounded on the door with her fists. "Help! Please help us."

A dog barked from somewhere inside the house, but no one came to the door.

"Let's try next door." She took the boy's hand and pulled him around the hedge dividing the two yards.

At that same moment, a car sped toward them from the same direction where Dazzle had driven. It was black… boxy…and an SUV.

Brooke didn't think her heart could pound any harder than it already was, but it jumped to a feverish tempo as she grabbed Cage by the wrist, turned, and ran away from the approaching vehicle.

They were three houses away from the corner when the black SUV skidded to at stop the curb.

99

AMBER

mber drove east, toward Hillview Terrace, a black SUV screamed past, going in the opposite direction. She wasn't sure, but she thought the license plate matched the one she had for Monroe Peck, aka Dazzle.

She whipped her steering wheel, turning into a driveway and out again, to pursue the fast-moving SUV.

The black vehicle took a left at the first cross street.

Amber followed, checking the area as she reached the stop sign, but there was no SUV or any other movement on the street. *Did he turn? How did he get out of sight so fast?* She drove to the next cross street and looked both left and right. No sign of the black vehicle. *Maybe he saw me and pulled into a driveway on that first street. Damn! You should have listened to Roy and requested an air unit.* Making another U-turn, she returned to the first street she'd passed.

As she came around the corner and skidded to a stop, anxiety filled Amber at the sight before her. The black SUV was parked at an angle, toward the curb. Both the driver's and the front passenger doors were wide open. In a residential front yard, a male Black had the left arm of a girl of about ten or eleven in an aggressive grip. He was pulling her toward the SUV. Amber recognized Monroe Peck from his mug shots.

When he spotted Amber, he pulled a gun out and pointed it at the little girl.

On the sidewalk, a Hispanic girl dragged Gage by the wrist toward the black vehicle.

Amber positioned her car to obstruct the suspects from fleeing, shoved the driver's side door open, and drew her gun, positioning herself behind the door as if she were in a patrol car. She had her sights fixed on the female gripping Gage's wrist. "Police! Let go of the children and put your hands up!"

"Fuck you, bitch," Peck yelled, glancing at the Hispanic female. "Get the kid in the car."

Amber's heart sank as the reality of her stupidity hit— hard. She had no backup, no radio to call for help, and no one knew her location. But she wasn't about to let these assholes drive off with her son.

She used every ounce of command presence she possessed and made sure the female saw the gun pointed at her. "Lady, I'm telling you to let go of the boy."

"Eden, she's not going to shoot you. You're unarmed."

The female hesitated. "That hasn't stopped cops before."

"Damn it, Eden, move your lazy ass!"

"Mama!"

Hearing Gage scream out for her twisted Amber's heart, and she hesitated.

That split second was all the Hispanic girl needed. She opened the rear passenger door and lifted a screaming Gage into the backseat, and then slammed the door shut.

"Mama! Mama!" Gage pounded on the window with open hands.

Amber turned the gun toward the male. "Let go of the little girl."

He grinned, inching closer to the SUV with Brooke as his shield. "Not gonna happen. Eden, take Kitty and put her in with the boy, then come back to me."

The female took the little girl from Peck's grasp and walked her around to the other side of the SUV, presumably to avoid Gage, who stood sobbing and crying for his mother at the window.

Once the little girl was secured, Peck told Eden to return to his side, and she did. "Now, I'm going to get into my car and drive away. And you're not going to follow me."

"That's not gonna happen," Amber said. "Any minute, this place is going to be flooded with cops. You need to give yourself up."

"I don't know who in the hell you are, lady, but if the cops were coming, they'd be here by now." A demented grin covered his face. "Put your gun on the street."

Amber shook her head. "No."

"I *said* put down your gun."

"That's not happening."

Rage replaced the maniacal smile on Peck's face. "You think I'm playin'?" He reached out and shot Eden in the head.

The girl dropped, blood puddling under her head and running into the gutter.

Amber fired at Peck skimming his shoulder. She watched as he ran behind the vehicle and jumped into the driver's seat. "Damn it!" She didn't dare fire again with Gage and the little girl in the rear seat.

Peck gunned the engine and sped past her as she scrambled back behind the wheel of her car and gave chase.

100

———————

ROY

Roy and Duke raced east on the 210 Freeway.

"Thank God, we were coming back from Palmdale, and didn't pass the 210 exchange," Duke said.

Roy nodded but said nothing, keeping his eyes focused on the roadway as he weaved in and out of the freeway traffic.

"There's the air unit…about two o'clock," she said.

He glanced at the sky and saw the LAPD airship heading east as well.

Duke took their portable radio and switched it over to the Foothill Division frequency.

Immediately, there was a transmission from the helicopter. "Air 11, I've got a black SUV, eastbound on Sunland, at Johanna Ave, being followed by a silver Lexus at a high rate of speed. We need some black-and-whites up here, Code 3."

Radio chatter exploded as Foothill patrol units responded.

"Yes!" Roy yelled. "We're coming up to the Sunland offramp. The silver Lexus is Amber. We'll be able to take over the pursuit."

The dispatcher broke in. "Attention all units, additional on the two vehicles eastbound Sunland. We've got a female on the line advising she is a plainclothes LAPD officer driving the silver Lexus. She advises the suspect is armed and dangerous and wanted for kidnapping and a possible 187. She also advises there are two juvenile kidnap victims in the back seat of the SUV."

"Who did Peck attempt to kill?" Duke murmured. "Do you think it was Amber?"

The dispatcher then came back on the air, assigning a Foothill unit to a possible 187 homicide that had just occurred on Hillview Terrace.

"Sounds like Peck dumped somebody before going on the run," Roy said. "Activate our red light, and I've got the siren. Hold on. I'm coming off the freeway hot."

Luckily, they had the green light as they skidded off the freeway, eastbound, onto Sunland Boulevard.

"Air 11, the suspect vehicle and the Lexus are passing under the 210 Freeway, and it looks like an unmarked police vehicle is joining the pursuit. All vehicles are approaching Wyngate."

"Air 11, the suspect is southbound Wyngate—standby, he's entered the apartment complex southeast corner of

Sunland and Wyngate. Suspect bailed and is on foot south-east through the buildings. Maroon shirt, black jeans."

Roy had just driven under the 210 Freeway overpass.

"Air 11, the driver of the Lexus, a white female, gray shirt and black jeans is approaching the black SUV. The male suspect is running north through the buildings and approaching the pool."

A Foothill patrol unit advised they were about two minutes out.

Roy looked at Duke. "Get ready. I'm going to drop you off with Amber and the kids, and I'll go on the other side of the apartment complex to try to intercept Peck."

Duke said nothing, just nodded and unhooked her seatbelt.

They turned southbound, on Wyngate, and thirty feet later, Roy skidded to a stop.

Duke jumped out and ran down the driveway of the apartment complex.

"Air 11, the suspect ran north of the pool and is now eastbound, about to exit the apartment complex onto Newhome Avenue."

Roy accelerated down Wyngate, praying it crossed Newhome.

"Air 11, to the plainclothes unit, turn north on Newhome, and the suspect should cross right in front of you. He's walking now, not running. Maroon shirt, black pants."

Roy followed the air ship's directions and seconds later, a lone male wearing a maroon shirt and black pants came into view crossing the street.

Roy, with his red light still visible, and his siren sounding, accelerated.

The male turned, pulled a gun, and began firing at the detective car.

Roy stomped on the gas pedal and sped toward the suspect who still fired at him. The impact was swift.

Peck was launched up and over the hood and into the air.

"Air 11, we need an RA for vehicle versus ped at Newhome south of Sunland."

The dispatcher acknowledged the request for a rescue ambulance.

Roy pulled to the curb, grabbed the portable radio, and ran back to Peck's body, which was bent at awkward angles and lifeless. He quickly felt for a pulse. "5K50, the suspect is a male twenty-five to thirty years, not conscious but breathing. Appears to have multiple fractures and contusions."

"5K50, roger."

A patrol unit arrived and began setting up a crime scene.

Roy's cell phone rang. "Amber?"

"I've got Gage! He seems to be okay. She dyed his hair red, and he won't let go of me, but I think he's okay."

"I'll be there as soon as I can. I'll be tied up with Force Investigation for a while, but I'll be there as soon as I can."

"Yeah, we're all in for a long night. I witnessed Peck killing one of his working girls. I'll stay in touch."

"Amber?"

"Yeah."

"Don't let our little boy out of your sight."

"Count on it."

EPILOGUE

F*our months later*

Roy sat on the sofa and patted the cushion next to him. "It's almost time."

Amber came from the kitchen, a generously filled glass of iced tea in each hand.

"Are you sure you want to watch it?" he asked.

She shrugged. "We lived through it, so I should be able to watch."

"Did you have any trouble getting Gage to go to bed?"

"No, none at all. I think therapy sessions, combined with getting the dog and wearing Gage out during the day, are finally allowing him to sleep at night without nightmares."

He smiled at her. "The therapist told me he might eventually forget all he saw and what happened to him."

Amber handed Roy his glass and sat next to him. "I hope so." She sighed. "I wish it were as easy for us."

He took her hand and raised it to his lips. "Honey, we managed to make it through the last four years. We can handle anything life is going to throw at us."

"I know you're right, and I *do* think our therapy is helping."

He smiled. "I do, too." His gaze flicked to the television. "Okay, here we go."

The somber investigative news reporter told the story of how two sisters, Brooke and Payton Desmond, from Boise, Idaho, were lured from their home by a ruthless pimp and the journey they had with him, leaving them damaged both physically and emotionally. "Payton was beaten and left for dead on the street, with Brooke clueless as to what had happened to her sister."

The story then shifted to the kidnapping of three-year-old Gage Buckner. "A prominent Hollywood casting director seemed to lose her grasp on reality when she was spurned by the boy's father, Detective Roy Buckner."

The reporter detailed Amber's police background and Roy and Amber's separation, which led to meeting Robyn McGee

"Gage Buckner was kidnapped in an elaborate plot, in which casting director Robyn McGee arranged for a staged car accident and gained her access to the Buckner child.

"McGee confessed to dressing as a man, and removing Gage Buckner from his mother's car, and placing him in her own vehicle several blocks away. She admitted drugging the child and leaving him in the cargo compartment of her vehicle, while she changed into a dress at a nearby hotel to establish and alibi with her appearance in the Justin Lowe homicide/rape case. The same case in which Detective Roy Buckner was a key prosecution witness."

Roy and Amber watched the actors play out the story they'd lived.

The reporter's face took on an expression of disgust. "When we come back, the story takes an unexpected twist when Gage Buckner is kidnapped…for a second time."

The show broke for a commercial.

Roy looked at Amber. "How are you holding up?"

"Okay, I guess." She made a face. "It's harder than I thought to relive it."

"I know." He sighed.

The show started again.

"When police stormed McGee's home, certain they would find Gage, but the child was nowhere in the home. It was later learned that he'd been kidnapped from McGee's house by one of her gardeners. Jaime Acosta, who is a member of a notorious local gang, took the child to sell for human trafficking purposes." The reporter's voice took on an ominous tone. "That's when things got really interesting." Antonio and his sister Araceli appeared on the screen.

Araceli talked about Victims of the Street and how it had turned her life around. She spoke about how not only Payton but also Sugar and Diamond had been rescued as well.

As the final day of Gage's kidnapping was reenacted, Amber held Roy's hand.

Snippets of news reports from that day flickered, one after another, and fancy graphics showed Dazzle murdering Eden, the pursuit, and its conclusion as Monroe Peck had fired fourteen rounds at Roy and how the detective had neutralized the threat by speeding toward his assailant and hitting him with his vehicle.

The reporter's voice deepened. "Monroe Peck died at the scene." The show broke for another commercial.

When it resumed, the reporter had a brighter tone in his voice. "So, where are they now?" Film footage of Payton and Brooke in Los Angeles at the Los Angeles Civilian Valor Awards with their parents, accepting medals for saving Gage, popped on the screen before switching to footage of the girls back at home, in Idaho, attending school and going to church with their parents.

In her interview, Payton said she wanted to start a program like Victims of the Street when she graduated high school. "With social media, it's so easy for pimps to find teens and work their way into vulnerable kids' lives. My pimp was smooth and reassuring. He had an answer for every concern I had." She looked directly into the camera. "If it can happen to me, it can happen to you."

Brooke said that she wanted to become a journalist and share the story of how easily young people were swept away into a lifestyle where they were basically slaves.

Finally, the reporter revealed his interview with Amber and Roy. "This horrific story does have a happy ending for your family, however. I'm told that the two of you renewed your wedding vows last month, and that you have another little one on the way."

On the screen, Amber smiled.

At home on her couch, Amber glared at the television. "I sure would like to know how he learned about the pregnancy."

Roy shrugged. "What difference does it make? Remember, Doctor Stevens says we're not supposed to sweat the small stuff."

"You know me, Roy. I like privacy and need to be in control. That way, none of us are in danger or will suffer from anymore damage."

He laughed. "Think about the last few years and everything we've been through. If anyone knows about danger, it's us…and we've proven we're experts at damage control." He pulled her into his arms and kissed the top of her head. "I love you, Amber."

"I love you, too, Roy."

* * *

Turn the page for insight into why this book was written, and the challenges I faced with the story.

AUTHENTIC CRIME...ARRESTING STORY

If you're reading this section before you've read the book, STOP! Read the story first. I'm about to reveal spoilers for Damage Control.

Damage Control is the third and final book in the Buckner trilogy.

This book touches on topics that makes many people squirm. Most people don't want to think about children being kidnapped, or being sexually exploited, and that's understandable. But as hard as it is to believe, there are people who don't know that these kinds of crimes exist.

In one of my first books, A Deadly Blessing, sexually exploited teens were part of the story. I got several reviews, but also emails from people saying: Thank you for writing this book. I didn't know this kind of thing goes on.

Which made me realize I can reach those folks by writing exciting stories with interesting and sympathetic characters—hopefully, without the story sounding "preachy." In doing so, I hope to share the knowledge to be aware of your surroundings, be cautious around people who approach you, and most importantly…know your children's friends, and where they're hanging out.

It was a difficult balance to not have the experiences of Brooke, Payton, and Dazzle overshadow the story of Gage Buckner. It was even harder to figure out a way to marry those two plot lines together, for what I hope was a satisfying and exciting ending.

In this book more than any other (to date), I took more procedural liberties…in other words, there are things that happened in this book regarding police procedures that would never happen in real life.

Although I suspect it was a tough read, I hope the angst, exploitation, and the will to survive was unmistakable, and resulted in an authentic and arresting story.

Warm regards,

Kathy Bennett

* * *

Sign up for Kathy's monthly newsletter today and receive an electronic short story FREE.

Sign Up at: www.KathyBennett.com

ABOUT THE AUTHOR

Hi there!

I'm Kathy Bennett.

A little about me—I worked for the LAPD for twenty-nine years. Eight years were spent as a civilian employee, and I served twenty-one years as a police officer. While most of my career was spent in a patrol car, I also worked at the police academy as a firearms instructor, promoted to the position of a field training officer, then worked in the "War Room" as a crime analyst. I promoted again, this time to the position of Senior Lead Officer—where I was in charge of a basic car area within a geographic division. I've done a few stints undercover and was honored to be named Officer of the Year in 1997.

In my spare time, I started writing romance books. However, I wasn't really cut out to be a romance author—I'd forget to write the romance, but I was always killing off one or more characters in the book. After a few years, I realized I'd better write what I know: Authentic Crime… Arresting Stories. (Yeah, that catchy phrase is a part of my brand.) One of the books in my Deadly Thriller series, *A Deadly Blessing*, was chosen by Barnes and Noble as one of the best original Nook books of the year.

I live in Idaho with my husband and soul mate, who is also a retired LAPD officer. We have two entertaining and energetic Labrador retrievers, and one cat who isn't nearly as active or amusing, but he's loved just as much. I like to garden, exercise, and spend time with our daughter and her family. Life doesn't get much better than the one I'm living.

I'm always interested in my readers. Drop me a line and tell me a little about yourself. You can reach me at Kathy@ KathyBennett.com and know that I *do* write back—and it's me—not an assistant.

* * *

All of my novels are heavily proofed, professionally edited, and formatted by a skilled team of professionals. Should you find any errors, please contact me directly. It's my goal to present you with the best possible reading experience, and I appreciate your help in making that happen. You can contact me at Kathy@KathyBennett.com

* * *

DID YOU ENJOY DAMAGE CONTROL?

If you enjoyed *Damage Control*, you can show your appreciation by leaving a review on Amazon, Barnes & Noble, Apple Books, Kobo Store, BookBub or Goodreads. I'm always grateful when a reader takes time out of their day to comment on my novels.

If you *do* write a review, please be sure to email me at: Kathy@KathyBennett.com so I can express my gratitude.